Carl Schraubstadter

Photo-Engraving

A practical treatise on the production of printing blocks by modern

photographic methods

Carl Schraubstadter

Photo-Engraving

A practical treatise on the production of printing blocks by modern photographic methods

ISBN/EAN: 9783337383589

Printed in Europe, USA, Canada, Australia, Japan

Cover: Foto ©Andreas Hilbeck / pixelio.de

More available books at **www.hansebooks.com**

PHOTO-ENGRAVING.

A PRACTICAL TREATISE

ON THE PRODUCTION OF PRINTING BLOCKS BY
MODERN PHOTOGRAPHIC METHODS.

BY

CARL SCHRAUBSTADTER, JR.

PUBLISHED BY

C. SCHRAUBSTADTER, JR.,

SAINT LOUIS.

1892.

CONTENTS.

INTRODUCTION.

The many requests that I recommend some good manual on this subject led to my reading all obtainable. Aside from the fact that the best were written in foreign languages, none were found which I considered entirely satisfactory. Not that they were without great value, but none were up to date; some attempted concealments, some gave no information on points necessary to a clear understanding of the subject, and in others the arrangement was inconsequent, or the work the result not of actual practice but of experiments only. Yet, in my opinion, the most frequent fault was their undue length, the desire of the writers being apparently to show all the variations of the different methods of accomplishing the same end. As many of these had, even at the time of writing, been superseded, and others are now but seldom used, I thought it best to write a clear description of those methods only which have been sanctioned by usage in commercial establishments. Methods for which others slightly better might sometimes have been substituted, but which on account of economy, speed and general utility, have been widely adopted. In the belief that too much general information would tend to confuse the beginner, and that many different recipes would result in his trying all without becoming acquainted with the possibilities of any, I may have erred in the direction of undue brevity, or appear dogmatic. I will thank the reader to point out any errors I have committed. I have also omitted, as much as possible, all theoretical knowledge; not that I consider theory unessential, but it is facts which the beginner needs—a little knowledge being often a dangerous thing. After a practical acquaintance with the work, a thorough study of optics, chemistry and photography alone will enable the operator to obtain the best work and experiment intelligently. In a chapter devoted to this subject I have endeavored to concisely catalogue the difficulties experienced by beginners, together with the proper remedies.

Neither is this work offered as a substitute for experience. The utmost which can be accomplished by a text book is to prevent the experimenter from wasting his time and energy in fruitless places. Wherever possible, personal instruction by a practical man is recommended. Learning from a book alone is often the most expensive method.

Among the many friends to whom I am indebted for aid and advice in preparing this book are Messrs. Chas. Chetham, G. H. Frommann and Lon Sanders.

C. S., JR.

CHAPTER I.

HISTORICAL SKETCH.

FROM its beginning the art of printing has been quick to avail itself of all advances in science and art. Often, indeed, experiments were conducted to a successful issue long before the conditions were such as warranted the introduction of the results from a commercial standpoint. This is particularly true of photo-engraving. In the strict sense of the word, photography is a printing process, but the general understanding of printing is a production of copies by means of ink and pressure. The various methods and processes are so closely connected, and in so many ways run into each other, that an exact nomenclature is almost impossible. To add to the difficulty, the experiments in photo-engraving, conducted over such a long period, and by so many experimenters in different parts of the globe, have resulted in a confusion of terms, which can only be simplified by time and usage. Aside from pure photography, in which the duplication is accomplished by sensitizing a suitable material and exposing it to the action of light beneath a negative, photography has been applied to all existing forms of printing, to a greater or less extent resembling the simpler printing methods. Thus we have Artotypy, Photo-lithography, Woodburytype, Photo-gravure, and other methods of producing intaglio engravings, corresponding closely to the copper plate method. All these, however, are of little use to the practical printer, as the engravings cannot be printed in a type form. Only of late years have the conditions been such as would admit of the production of relief engravings by the aid of photography.

As before noted, confusion of nomenclature makes it difficult to give good definitions. Photo-relief engraving perhaps expresses the idea better than any other term, but, aside from its awkwardness and length, confining it to its strict sense necessarily excludes such methods as do not directly avail themselves of the action of light, and as the modern processes are to a great extent the results of experiments in this direction, and the operator is called upon to use them, the term must be set aside. Chemigraphy, a word proposed by a number of German authors, and to a certain extent adopted on the continent, presents the objection that, among others, lithography is also a chemical process. Amongst the English-speaking artists the word "Process" has been largely adopted to distinguish all photographic methods from wood engraving. This term has taken some root amongst the English printers, but as photo-engraving can hardly be said to be more of a "process" than wax engraving, it is hardly applicable. The term generally sanctioned by usage is "Photo-engraving." Though by some extended so as to cover all methods of photo-reproduction, and by others used to distinguish the gelatine processes from zinc etching, it is widely and generally used to include such processes only as produce relief plates, and it is in this sense that it will be used throughout this work. Zinc etching is the method of producing a relief printing plate by protecting the surface of the lines, and removing the rest of the metal so as to leave them in relief. Generally the drawing is reproduced on the metallic plate by means of photography, and this method has been called photo-zinc etching or photo-zinc engraving, in distinction from that process in which the drawing is made by the artist directly upon the surface of the metal. Copper and other metals are sometimes substituted for the zinc, but it is rarely spoken of as copper etching, the term zinc etching being generally used to include these variations. The acid resisting coating is sometimes made by covering the metal with a thin sheet of asphaltum and exposing it beneath a negative, the parts reached by the light being rendered insoluble in turpentine, and remaining on development. Usually the surface is sensitized by albumen, or other organic matter, in combination with bichromate of potash or ammonia, the process being based on the insolubility of such substances in cold water after exposure to the light. This property is also made use of in the photo-gelatine washout method, usually referred to simply as the washout process, in which a sheet of gelatine sensitized with one of these chrome salts is exposed beneath a suitable negative. The soluble portions are afterwards washed away,

giving a relief plate. Another property of bichromatized gelatine is the loss of its tendency to swell by absorbing water after
exposure to light. In the gelatine swell method this is taken
advantage of, the lines being hardened by the action of light,
and the surrounding spaces afterwards brought into relief by
soaking in water. Plaster casts, and afterwards a metal cast,.
produce a relief plate suitable for the press. The term half-
tone, as applied to relief engravings of a certain class, is hardly
satisfactory, but its universal adoption will not permit the sub-
stitution of another word. This is a photographic method by
which a printing plate is produced in relief from a photograph or
painting in which there are no lines or dots, but simply a grada-
tion of tints. There are a number of ways of producing the
lines or dots necessary in such engravings, but almost universally they are made by intervention of a screen plate between
the copy and the sensitized plate. From the line or stipple
negative, a drawing or relief block may be made by any of the
above methods, although zinc etching is generally selected.

It is a curious fact that Niepce, the originator of photography
and the co-worker of Daguerre, made his first experiments with
asphaltum, a substance which is to-day used for obtaining the
finest photo-engravings, and that the object of these experiments was the production of a printing plate. In 1824 he made
a picture in a camera obscura, in which the image was produced
on a silver plate coated with asphalt. Shortly afterwards he
is said to have etched some of these plates in relief. In recent
times, Dr. Kaysar has promulgated the present method of in-
creasing the sensitiveness of the asphaltum. A process of
etching daguerreotypes so as to produce printing plates was set
forth by Grove in 1841, and shortly after, Berra attempted to
produce printing plates by a similar method. These plates, however, were too shallow to be of much value. Probably the first
practical use of such engravings was for illustrating "Le
Journel Amusant" in Paris. In 1847 Niepce de St. Victor,
nephew of Daguerre's partner, succeeded in sensitizing an albumen film on glass. During the 50's numerous experiments
were made throughout Europe. In 1851 collodion, suggested
by Legray, was practically applied by Archer. In 1852 Fox
Talbot, whose discoveries in photography were made public
even before those of Niepce and Daguerre, obtained a patent

for a process in which steel plates were coated with bichromate of potash and gelatine. After exposure beneath a negative the soluble gelatine was washed off and the plate etched into relief by bichloride of platinum. It will be seen that this method closely resembles modern zinc etching. In 1859 Poitevin at Paris, and Pretch in Vienna, applied for patents based on the fact that gelatine treated with certain chrome salts, after exposure to the light, loses its property of absorbing water and swelling. They experimented with a method similar to the gelatine swell process of to-day. Pretch obtained a patent in that year and Poitevin, in 1855, and about the same time Pretch also succeeded in producing a grained plate, obtaining very fair results. Shortly afterwards Fox Talbot made use of the other properties of bichromatized gelatine, namely its impermeability and its insolubility in water after exposure to light. Thomas Sutton and John Pouncy also experimented in 1858. In 1859 Osborne in Australia, and Asser in Holland, simultaneously introduced the method of photographing on transfer paper, developing the image with fatty ink and transferring this image to stone. Sir Henry James soon after transferred to zinc. In 1859 a patent was taken out in Austria for photo-lithography, the print being made directly on the stone by asphalt and developed with turpentine. Amongst others, Falk, Schippang, Lea, Kronheim, Fontaine, Placet, Swan and Vogel afterwards contributed towards the perfection of the different methods. While some good results were obtained, commercial success had been achieved by none, and it was not until the Austrian Government commenced its series of experiments that modern photoengraving became a permanent success. At first these experiments were conducted by Pretch, who on account of his age and failing faculties did not even succeed in duplicating his former achievements. In 1873 Prof. Husnik took his place and succeeded in producing practical printing plates. At this time experimenters throughout the civilized world were beginning to take renewed interest in photo-engraving. The gelatine swell process was perfected so that fair results were obtainable, and photo-lithography was also brought to a practical basis. Long before this experiments had been made with a view to producing a relief printing plate by means of etching. In 1789 and afterwards, the talented and eccentric artist, Wm.

Blake, illustrated "The Book of Thel" and "The Songs of In-
nocence" by drawing his designs on copper with acid-resisting
ink and etching out the white spaces with aquafortis. Blake
claimed that the method and the ink were revealed to him by
his deceased brother's spirit. Senefelder's first experiments
were with the idea of producing a relief plate by drawing on
the surface of a stone with an acid-resisting ink and etching
out the white spaces. Had he been successful it is possible
that lithography of to-day would still be unknown. A number
of experimenters paved the way for the present zinc etching
method. During the 60's a process was attempted in which
the metal was covered with an etching ground. On this the
design was scratched. The plate was then subjected to the
action of acid, producing a sunken engraving. After cleaning,
the lines were filled with solder or with a mixture of asphaltum
and ink, as for printing a copper plate, and the plate again
etched, bringing the lines into relief. There were many varieties of this process. In one of them the scratched plate was
hung in the battery, and gold or other acid-resisting metal de-
posited on the lines, so that the etching could be made. After
the first etch, acid-resisting ink was applied to the plate and
rubbed off with a circular motion so that enough was left to
protect the sides of the lines during the subsequent etch. The
results, however, were hardly satisfactory. The first successful application of photography to zinc etching was by the use
of transfer paper, an offshoot of photo-lithography. A sheet of
paper coated with bichromatized gelatine was exposed beneath
a negative and inked with a lithographic roller. On rubbing
it while beneath water, the ink was removed from all such portions as had not been exposed to the light. The transfer to
the polished zinc plate was then made in an ordinary lithographic press.

The next step of improvement was the direct printing on
zinc. Although the asphalt method was one of the earliest in
use for etching, and Talbot had used bichromatized gelatine on
steel, it was not until the bichromatized albumen solution with
a coating of ink was adopted that the product became a commercial article. The greatest difficulty was experienced in protecting the sides of the lines so that a good relief could be obtained without losing the more delicate lines of the drawing.

Numerous methods were proposed, and a number put to practical use. The experimenters may be counted not only by
hundreds but by thousands, and as many endeavored to keep
their methods secret, the amount of credit due to each is hard
to determine. Even now it is difficult to obtain access to the
best establishments, and almost every engraver has his own
methods and recipes, but the change of workmen from one
situation to another, and the tendency, every year more apparent, to formulize facts and abolish mystery have tended to
eliminate the less practical methods, so that the processes employed by the various photo-engravers do not essentially differ.
To trace the development of the art would involve not only a
history of photography, but of lithography and wood and copper
engraving as well. The scope of this work will not permit
even an attempt in this direction.

Probably the first zinc etching in America was done by
Chas. Henry, a Frenchman, who came to this country in 1865
and formed a partnership with a wood engraver named Arnold.
The method used was that of making a photographic print on
lithographic transfer paper, transferring it to the surface of a
plate and etching it with sulphuric acid. The results were not
altogether satisfactory, and the partnership was soon dissolved,
Henry afterwards entering into the employ of Frank Leslie.
Renewed interest in the process, and the gradual solution of
difficulties which (though apparently small and unimportant to
one unfamiliar with engraving) stood in the way of success,
induced many practical men to engage in the business. A
glance at the trades' papers of the last decade will show the ex-
traordinary progress of the art, both as to the number of firms
engaged in the business and the quality of the work.

CHAPTER II.

ARRANGEMENT AND EQUIPMENT OF THE SHOP.

Unless erected expressly for the purpose, a good workshop is difficult to find. With slight alteration, an old photographic studio will answer very well. As these are seldom located in the right district, a light room, preferably at the top of a building, with the ceilings and windows as high as possible, is to be chosen. A skylight, though expensive, is a most profitable investment. Where circumstances warrant the necessary outlay, an arc electric lamp will render the operator independent of daylight. Whenever practicable, a separate room should be used for each department, such as photographing, etching and finishing. It is absolutely necessary that the dark room should be kept separate from the other working space, and, if possible, also the etching and photographing. On the next page (Fig. 1) are plans for a shop having all modern conveniences, and adapted to doing a great deal of work economically. In this arrangement the photographing room is far enough away to keep out all dust, dirt, and disturbances made by the other departments.

In general, it will be noted that running water is desirable in most of the rooms, and it is most economical to have the sinks close together. Next to the photographers, the artists and finishers require the best light, and where there is no skylight for them, the north wall is best, as there is no direct sunlight during any part of the day. As the etchers also require good light, the tubs should be placed close to the windows. In the photographing room, shown at the northwest corner, may be seen two cameras, 1, hung on swings, with the electric light, 2, between them; 3 represents the reflector; 4, bench for tacking up copy, etc.; while the dotted lines show the outline of the skylight; 5 is the case for chemicals; 6, compounding table; and 7, a sink for intensifying negatives, having a small bench at its side.

Above all, select a portion of a building which is solid. The vibration of machinery, and even of passing wagons, will, in some buildings, disturb the camera so that no compensating

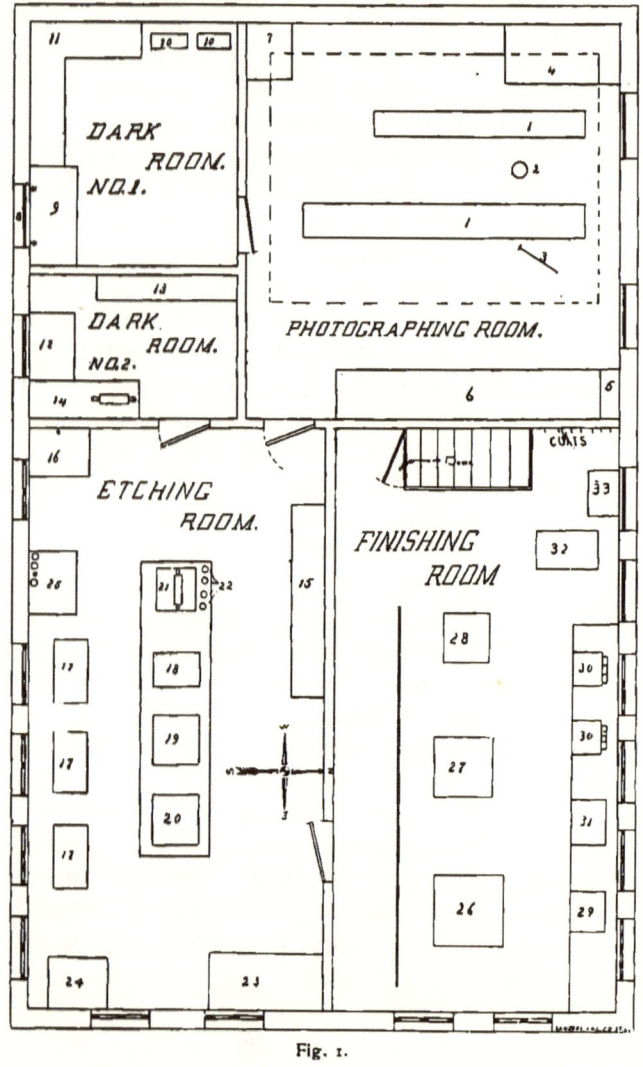

Fig. 1.

device will make the negatives perfect. The ceiling and walls should be painted or whitewashed light gray, and the floor painted some dark color. The size of room will depend upon the nature of the work and the number of operators. For a

14x17 inch camera, a 12-foot slide is not too long, consequently there should be room to place this in a good position. The lighting is of the utmost importance. Wherever possible, a skylight should be let into the ceiling. This should be a trifle longer than the camera swing, and wide enough to accommodate the

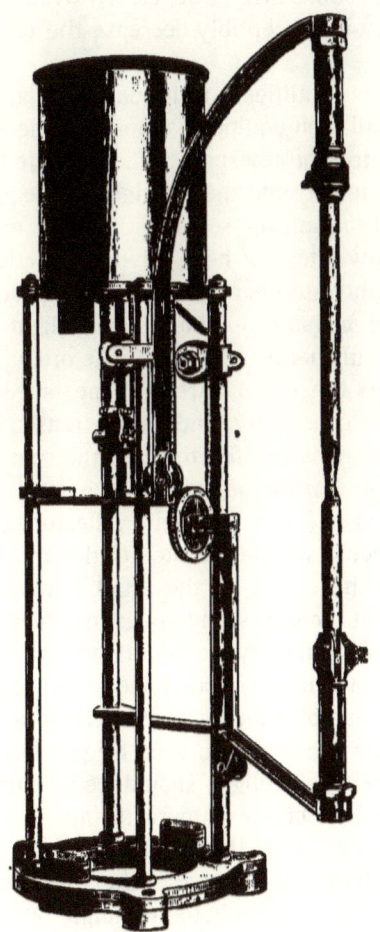

Fig. 2.

number of cameras used. Thus, for a gallery running one camera 10 x 12 and one 14 x 17, the skylight should be about 10 x 14 feet. Its shape and construction will of course depend upon the building, but the larger the better. If possible, it should slant at an angle of 15 to 30 degrees towards the north, as this will provide against direct sunlight upon the copying board for the greater part of the day. The panes of glass should be large, so that the cross-bars will not cut off the light. They should lap each other as little as possible, an eighth of an inch being sufficient. Use clear, white glass. A slight yellowish tint will perceptibly decrease the actinic power of the light.

In very few localities can the daylight be depended upon, and therefore all well equipped shops use electric light. This is particularly true of newspaper offices where the work is done entirely after sunset, and the skylight consequently dispensed with. Though requiring somewhat longer exposure, electric light has the advantage of being always exactly the same, thus enabling the photographer to time his exposure much better than with the constantly changing sunlight. Incandescent lamps are not sufficiently intense. The ordinary arc lamp will answer, but, as the upper carbon alone is fed, the position of the arc changes constantly, and for this reason a focusing lamp, in which the carbons are fed towards the center, is preferable, as it will always throw the light in the same direction. Such a lamp is shown in Fig. 2. A metal reflector eight or ten inches in diameter should be placed back of the arc. The lamp may be hung from the ceiling in the usual manner, or, better still, placed on a light wooden stand about four feet high, so that the direction of the light may be regulated. It will generally be found most economical to purchase from some electric light company, but establishments having their own incandescent plants can make use of the current by purchasing a converter. Running across the skylight should be a beam strong enough to bear the weight of the camera swings. The construction shown in Fig. 3 is preferable. The cross beam should be as small as consistent with strength, otherwise the shadow thrown by it may interfere with photographing. A wire rope is preferable, as it will wear longer. The swing should be adjusted so that the operator will not have to assume an inconvenient position. A height which will make the center of the camera come six inches below his chin will be found about right. The slides should be about a quarter of an inch wider than the base of the camera, so as to allow it to move easily.

The following table gives the length of bed for ordinary reductions:

For 8 x 10 inch camera, length of bed, 8 feet.
For 10 x 12 inch camera, length of bed, 9 feet.
For 11 x 14 inch camera, length of bed, 10 feet.
For 14 x 17 inch camera, length of bed, 12 feet.
For 17 x 20 inch camera, length of bed, 15 feet.
For 20 x 24 inch camera, length of bed, 20 feet.

Fig. 3.

The purpose of a swing is to guard against vibration, the copy board and camera moving together if disturbed. Most operators prefer to have the end on which the copy board rests

Fig. 4.

slightly lower, so that the latter will be kept in position by gravity. As shifting the camera for various reductions changes the center of gravity, a movable weight may be provided for balancing. Generally, the copy-board holder shown in

Fig. 3 is provided. This may be fastened permanently to the swing, and the copy pinned directly upon it. Most operators prefer to pin their copy to another board with thumb tacks, and lay this board against the holder, as illustrated in Fig. 4. Where large drawings are to be copied in sections, a holder which will permit the copy-board being slid across the swing without changing the focus is preferable. Where circumstances do not warrant the outlay of a skylight or an electric light, the stand illustrated in Fig. 4 will be found desirable, as it can be moved around to accommodate the shifting light. Many operators who have fixed light prefer a stand to the swing, omitting the springs and substituting small rubber balls for the castors.

Of the utmost importance is the lens. This should be of the rectilinear type. A portrait lens will not answer. Beginners are apt to make the mistake of purchasing a cheap lens. It is far better to purchase a good one having a smaller field, even though an occasional large job has to be made in sections. The average job will be much smaller than 8 x 10 inches, and few are larger than 10 x 12. Used with a large diaphragm, a comparatively small lens will make a large picture, but the corners will not be sufficiently sharp to make a good print. Consequently it is stopped down by a small diaphragm. While this increases the sharpness, it diminishes the amount of light admitted, and consequently increases the length of exposure, and is liable to veil the lines. As the wet collodion process is altogether used, and the length of exposure limited to the time the sensitized plate will remain moist, the necessity of a lens which will make a clear picture when stopped with a medium diaphragm is apparent. This is particularly true in summer, when evaporation takes place rapidly. There are many different makes of lenses. Amongst the best are the Dallmeyer, Steinheil, Voigtlander, Ross and Taylor & Hobson. If possible, purchase a lens from some reliable concern, with the privilege of returning unless satisfactory. If you can procure the assistance of an experienced photographer in making the tests, so much the better. If not, hold the lens in the hand and look through the aperture at a piece of paper tinted light blue. If wrongly constructed, it may have "ghosts," which will be visible in the form of mist or fog which appears to be in the glass. If such is the case, the lens should be rejected. If perfectly clear, it should be tested for speed, covering power, accuracy in copying straight lines, intensity and equal distribution of light. These points may be settled by making a negative, but before rejecting it be sure that the fault is in the lens and not in your chemicals, light, other apparatus, or the lack of photographic knowledge.

The ordinary copying camera, illustrated in Fig. 5, fitted

Fig. 5.

with long bellows and cone, is generally used.   10 x 12 and 11 x 14 will be found the most convenient sizes.   The lens should be fastened exactly in the center of the lens board, a hole being bored to fit it, and the edges of the wood blackened to correspond with the interior of the camera.   The ground glass should be without perceptible grain, and when placed in the camera should come in precisely the same position that the sensitized plate will afterwards occupy.   To determine this, take out the lens board, and measure the distance between the front of the camera and the glass.   It should be exactly the same from each of the four corners.   Then remove the ground glass and insert in its place the plate holder containing the largest size glass it will admit.   Pull out the slide, and measure as before, when the distance should be exactly the same.   The old style plate holders are provided with kits to fit various sizes of glass.   They have been almost entirely superseded by the modern Bonanza and Benster holders, which need not be described here. The enlarging and reducing camera shown in Fig. 6 resembles the

Fig. 6.

other, and can be used in the same manner, but the lens can also be placed in the interior of the camera, and a transparency in the front. This arrangement is by some preferred for making half tone negatives, and also for making large silver prints. Though constructed on the same principles, there is a great difference in the quality of the various makes of cameras, and they should always be purchased from some dealer of reputation.

The operating room should be provided with a table for tacking copy to the board. Near the dark room there should be a sink with running water, and along side of this a bench provided with rubber trays, etc., for intensifying and fixing negatives, as also for cleaning the negative glasses. Beneath the sink should be placed the tub for receiving the used negatives. On the outside of one of the windows which has a good light should be placed a stout shelf twelve or fifteen inches wide, on which the printing frames for making silver prints and the extra silver bath may be placed. In establishments having electric light a table of suitable height may be used for exposing the prints on zinc. This will be spoken of at length further on.

Nothing but the chemicals and apparatus in actual use should be placed in the dark room No. 1, which opens from the operating room, and which is intended for making negatives only. Again referring to Fig. 1, 8 represents a window; 9, the sink; 10, bath holders, and 11, shelves. The room should be large enough to work in comfortably. Six by eight feet will do very well, but eight by ten is not too large. Where there are a number of operators it will be best to have a small room for each, as during the occupancy of the room the door must not be opened. In one end there should be a window glazed with orange glass. If the situation is such that direct sunlight enters at any time while the room is being used, an awning or curtain should be provided. If the ceilings and walls are whitewashed, they had best be scraped and painted a light yellow. If of wood, they should be shellaced or varnished. In place of the paint and varnish, the glazed wall paper used for bath rooms will answer very nicely. Beneath the window should be erected a suitable sink. Its dimensions will vary according to size and quantity of work, but it is best to err in making it too large than too small. The depth should be about eight inches, the width may be anything from eighteen to thirty inches, and the length, from four to six feet. Above it should be two faucets connecting with the water main, one of them provided with rubber hose and a rose jet. Where there are no water connections, a galvanized iron reservior may be provided, and for experimental purposes, two whiskey barrels, one above the other, the upper one provided with a faucet arranged so as to drain into the lower. Where it is impracticable to place a window in the dark room, artificial light may be used. A gas argand burner with yellow chimney will do very nicely. An oil lamp can also be used, but those sold by photographic stock houses for dry plate work give too feeble a light. A large lamp protected by heavy orange glass·is conducive to good work. For experimental work, the window may be covered with yellow "post office" paper, or an ordinary lamp or gas flame used behind a sheet of glass covered with the same material in such manner as to prevent any white rays from falling in the room. It is of the utmost importance that no daylight enter the dark room except through the orange glass. When it has been completed, the door should be closed, the window covered, and a careful examination made from every possible point of view. Every crack and crevice must be filled or covered, as the least white ray will play havoc with the plate. By the side of the sink should be placed a shelf for the accommodation of the work, and other shelves should also be placed on the sides of the walls to hold the plate holder, negative glass, developer, collodion vial and bottle, fixing tray and bath holder. For all except experimental work this last should be much larger than actually required.

The second dark room has no connection with the first, and is used for sensitizing and rolling up zinc plates only. It need not be so dark as the other. For experimental purposes, a dark corner of the room shut off by a yellow curtain will do, but direct sunlight must be excluded. In the diagram, 12 represents the work table on which is a gas stove for drying the plates; 13, the shelves for bottles, printing frame, etc.; 14, ink slab. The printing frame is kept in this room when not in use. It should be at least one inch larger each way than the negative it is desired to make. For the ink slab, a piece of marble or slate about twice the size of the largest sheet to be etched should be selected. It should be free from flaws or holes. A lithographic roller is generally used, though many prefer one of hard composition. The gas stove need not be large. An ordinary Bunsen burner can be made to answer, or an oil stove substituted. In the etching room, 15 is a bench for stripping negatives, etc.; 16 is the sink; 17, the etching tubs; and in the center is a bench on which is a furnace, 18; marble slab for cooling the plate, 19; powder box, 20; roller and slab for inking up the plate during etching, 21. At the back of the latter are cups for holding gum solution, water, sponge and ink, 22. The part on which the ink slab is placed is about thirty inches high, the rest, thirty-eight. One of the windows should be provided on the outside with a shelf for exposing prints on zinc. The sink need not be large, as it is used only for supplying the etching tubs with water and receiving the wastes. The number and size of the etching tubs will depend entirely upon the quantity and kind of work. For small establishments, an ordinary gas burner can be used in place of the oven, which will be described further on. An old lithographic stone or press bed will answer nicely for the cooling slab. An ordinary box will do for powdering, but one made especially for the purpose, and provided with a lid, is better. The reader is referred to following chapters for further description of these articles, as well as rollers, etc., used for gumming up. Many establishments omit the gumming operation, and the beginner need not purchase the materials. In most places the polishing of the zinc is also done in this room. 23 represents a table on which the zinc is cut to size, and on it is also an iron plate for leveling the zinc plates, a pair of callipers and a hammer. 24 is polishing stand with material, and 25, a bench or table for retouching the prints. In large establishments where the zinc is buffed, the buff is placed alongside the polishing table. Experimenters will do well to purchase their zinc already polished. In the finishing room, 26 represents the router; 27, the circular saw; and 28, the trimmer. The heavy line at the rear of these machines represents the main shaft, which connects with power from the floor below, or a motor. One-half horse-power each for the router and trimmer is sufficient, and one and a half or two-horse power for the saw, according to its construction and condition. As all these tools seldom run at one time, two-horse power will generally be found enough. Large establishments also run their etching tubs with power. At the north wall are the finishing benches, 29 being shoot board and plane; 30, blocking plates; 31, engraver's table. These benches are about thirty-four inches high. 32 is a proof press; and 33, table for paper, etc. The above plan cannot be followed closely except in rare instances, but must be changed according to circumstances. Details will be furnished in the following chapters, as well as descriptions of many smaller articles which have been omitted.

CHAPTER III.

PREPARATION OF CHEMICALS.

The collodion wet plate method is almost exclusively used for photo-engraving. Dry plates can be utilized, but the first cost, the fact that the glass cannot be used over again, the long time required for development, the necessity of excluding all but feeble red light from the dark room, the long washing which is requisite, and the difficulty in obtaining intensity detract from their desirability. The objections to the collodion method are, the comparatively long exposure required, the fact that every plate must be made immediately before using, that the making of these plates involves considerable skill and experience, and that the silver bath is liable to get out of order ; but these are not as serious as would at first appear. Unlike portrait photography, the object remains still, and therefore is not liable to make a blurred image, and while one plate is being exposed the operator can prepare another. A duplicate silver bath and a little experience will overcome the other objections, and if there were no other reason, economy alone would dictate its choice. The compounding of the various preparations used in photography should be done in the photographing room at a bench near the sink. Army scales, illustrated in Fig. 7, are accurate enough for the purpose. It is seldom necessary to weigh more than one ounce at a time, and weights from one grain up to one ounce Troy should be pro-

Fig. 7.

vided. Many prefer dispensing scales shown in Fig. 8, as they are easier to handle. If the business is such that preparations must frequently be made up, it is best to cut pieces of glass or metal into weights agreeing with quantities required. Paper labels should be pasted upon them, on which are written the

25

weight and the chemical to be weighed off ; thus, " Bromide of zinc 75 grains." This will save time in looking up formulæ and adding together small weights. Although all formulæ call for Troy ounces, containing 480 grains, chemicals are always sold

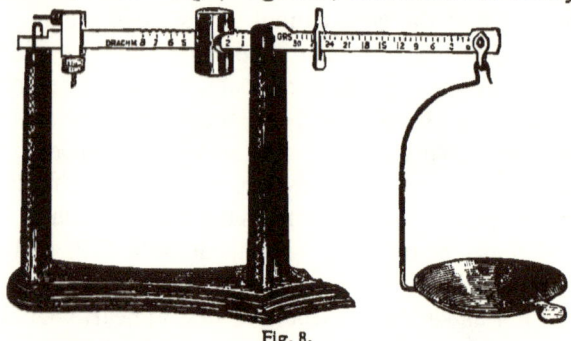

Fig. 8.

by Avoirdupois weight, an ounce having but 437½ grains. For measuring fluids, two graduates, three and sixteen ounce, should be purchased. Also two funnels, pint and half gallon (the latter reserved for the silver bath), and a funnel stand for holding them. It will not pay to economize on these, even in a small place. Better have three or four funnels of various sizes, and if one is reserved for each preparation it will pay in the end. Few photographers now use filtering paper. Absorbent cotton is cheaper, works more rapidly, is easier to use, and, except for special purposes which will be enumerated further on, just as good. A special silver hydrometer should be used for measuring the quantity of silver in the bath, and if it is desired to test the intensity of other liquids, hydrometers for liquids heavier or lighter than water can be obtained. All these articles should be kept on a shelf above the compounding bench.

The utmost care should be taken in the selection of the chemicals. Those sold by drug stores are seldom of the right quality. Procure them from some photo-engravers' supply establishment. Beginners are advised to purchase their preparations made up, as it will enable them to center their attention on the manipulation. Afterwards the formulæ may be obtained and the preparations made up as opportunity offers. Impure water is a frequent source of trouble. Usually tap water will answer very well, but if not clear it should always be filtered. If there is any doubt as to its purity, use distilled water, which costs very little.

COLLODION.

Collodion is generally made first, as it seldom works well when first prepared and always improves with age. The best way is to add to the pouring vial, every evening, a little collodion which has not yet been used, but has aged, or as photographers express it, "ripened," for several weeks. Almost every photographer has a recipe which he considers better than all others. If you know one who is producing good results for photo-engraving purposes, you need not hesitate to accept his formula under his guidance, but do not experiment with several before you are thoroughly acquainted with the possibilities of one. This is a mistake beginners are very apt to make. While the advice and assistance of an experienced collodion photographer are of much help, it should be remembered that the conditions of portrait and landscape photography are entirely different from those of photo-mechanical engraving.

The following is a recipe which has proven of worth in a number of establishments :

Alcohol, ...	15 ounces.
Ether, sulph. conc., ...	20 ounces.
Gun cotton, ...	280 grains.
Bromide of Zinc, ...	75 grains.
Iodide of Zinc, ...	175 grains.
Alcohol, ...	5 ounces.

Absolute alcohol is quite expensive, and many photographers use a good quality, 98 per cent. Wood alcohol will not answer. The ether should be concentrated sulphuric. There are a number of brands in the market, so it should not be purchased at a drug store. Almost all works on photography describe methods of making the gun cotton, which differs from the commercial article, being inexplosive and entirely soluble in alcohol and ether, but its preparation involves such care and experience that the photo-engraver would find it impossible to make a uniform article. Competition has brought down the price so that even the largest establishments now purchase instead of making it. The finer qualities, though costing a little more, will pay for themselves in the end, and are especially recommended to beginners. Cellodine is an excellent substitute. The zinc salts should be fresh and of the best quality. Take a seven-pound bottle, perfectly clean, and pour into it the amount of alcohol

given in the first half of the formula, then add the cotton or cellodine.   Shake well and stir occasionally, particularly if you
have used the latter, otherwise the cellodine will form a jelly-
like mass which is difficult to dissolve.   After a short time, add
the ether and shake well until there is no longer any undissolved
solid, then set away to clear.   Put the bromide of zinc in a glass
or porcelain mortar, which should be perfectly clean, and add a
few drops of alcohol so that you can grind it to a paste.   Continue to add alcohol until it has taken up as much bromide as it
will dissolve, allow it to settle a few moments and pour into a
clean sixteen-ounce bottle.   Continue adding alcohol and pouring it off until the bromide is entirely dissolved.   Do the same
thing with the iodide, for which there will be enough alcohol
left, unless too much has been used for the bromide.   If such is
the case, add a few drops of distilled water, but no more than
necessary.   The contents of the sixteen-ounce bottle, which
will appear somewhat milky, are now filtered into the plain collodion, which is then again well shaken and set aside for a few
days to settle.   When perfectly clear and transparent it may
be drawn off for use.   The following is another excellent recipe
which gives intense negatives and ripens somewhat quicker :

Alcohol, ...	20 ounces.
Ether, ...	20 ounces.
Gun cotton, ...	280 grains.
Iodide of Ammonium, ...	160 grains.
Bromide of Cadmium, ...	80 grains.
Chloride of Calcium, ...	80 grains.

It is prepared in exactly the same manner as the first, a few
ounces of the alcohol being reserved for dissolving the salts.

New collodion unmixed with old sometimes makes foggy
negatives.   Adding a few drops tincture of iodine (resublimed
iodine 1 ounce, alcohol 8 ounces), sufficient to make it a light
red color, will make it work free from fog, and yet give perfect
intensity.   Ether evaporates much more rapidly than alcohol.
If the collodion be too thick it should be thinned with concentrated sulphuric ether only.   It should, however, be thicker
than that used for portrait photography.   An excess of ether
makes a tough, horny film, but prevents intensity.   An excess
of alcohol makes the film rotten, but increases intensity.

THE SILVER BATH.

Every plate which is sensitized takes a certain amount of silver from the bath and adds impurities. For this reason the quantity and the holder should be as large as possible, so that the change will be slow. As it is liable to give out without a moment's warning, a duplicate bath of the same quantity should always be kept ready, unless you are confining yourself to experimental work and can afford to wait several days in case of a mishap. Though the first cost is more, a large bath is less expensive to run than a small one, as it will require less "doc-

toring." The bath holder, Fig. 9, should be of glass encased in a wooden box having a hinged cover. Porcelain will, however, answer nicely, but the hard rubber baths sometimes sold for this purpose are not desirable, as they quickly foul the bath. For the same reason a dipper of silver wire is preferable, but hard rubber is almost universally used. The nitrate of silver should be triple fused, as sold by supply houses for this purpose. Cheap grades contain impurities, and

Fig. 9.

are dear at any price. Pour into a large white bottle enough distilled water to fill your bath holder, add the nitrate of silver until sufficient has dissolved to make it register 40 grains to the ounce with the silver hydrometer. This may be observed by thoroughly shaking the contents and pouring a little of the solution into the tube which accompanies the hydrometer. Carefully place the latter into the tube, and when it floats quietly, note the figure at the surface of the liquid. If it registers below 40, nitrate of silver must be added; if above, more distilled water. Roughly, it will require about twelve ounces nitrate of silver to make one gallon of bath. When it registers correctly, test with a strip of blue litmus paper. If the color remains unchanged, and distilled water was not used, expose to the sun for a few days, when all organic impurities will be precipitated in the form of black powder. If the color of the litmus paper is changed to red, the silver was not properly made and contains free acid, in which case concentrated water ammonia should be added a few drops at a time, under constant stirring, until the paper is changed back to its blue color before exposing to the light. When clear, filter into the bath holder and add nitric acid, C. P., a few drops at a time, until the blue litmus paper dipped into it acquires a decidedly red color. Do not add too much acid and stir constantly while so doing.

Allow it to rest again for a few hours, when it will be ready for iodizing. This can be done by adding iodide of potash, but most photographers prefer to do so by coating a glass plate with collodion in exactly the same manner as if sensitizing it for a negative, and lowering it into the bath holder with the dipper. Directions for this will be found in the next chapter. The film will at first become translucent and creamy, but on removing it after a few hours will again be perfectly transparent, the bath having dissolved the salts from the collodion. One large plate is generally sufficient to iodize the bath, but, on trial, should the resulting negative be found of a bluish color and foggy in the lights the above operation must be repeated. Do not over iodize the bath until you are certain the fog is caused by it. Directions for correcting faulty baths will be given in Chapter V.

THE DEVELOPER.

Water, ...	16 ounces.
Sulphate of Iron, ...	1 ounce.
Acetic Acid No. 8, ...	2 ounces.
Alcohol, ...	1 ounce.

The sulphate of iron (sometimes called persulphate) and acetic acid should be of a high grade, but need not be chemically pure. Place the water in a bottle, add the iron and shake until it is dissolved, then add the acetic acid, shake again, and filter through a plug of absorbent cotton pushed into the neck of a funnel. After a few days this developer will become darker and sediment will form at the bottom. This will not impair its usefulness, though the sediment should be removed by filtering.

FIXING SOLUTION.

Cyanide of potassium, ...	1 ounce.
Water, ...	6 ounces.

The cyanide of potassium should be fused and of good quality. Break it up into small lumps and place it in a bottle with the water. Shake until dissolved, when it is ready for use. This solution loses strength from use, and should frequently be replaced with new. It is extremely poisonous, and the fumes, which are stronger in warm weather, should be avoided as much as possible.

INTENSIFIER.

No. 1.

Saturated solution bichloride of mercury, . . . 8 ounces.
Chloride of ammonium, ... 2 ounces.

Water is preferably distilled. The chemicals should be pure. A small amount of bichloride of mercury should always remain at the bottom of the stock bottle. When the water will take no more, add the chloride of ammonium, shake thoroughly and filter. This solution also is poisonous. It should be occasionally filtered, and strengthened by the addition of new solution.

No. 2.

Hydrosulphuret of ammonium, ... 1 ounce.
Water, ... 5 ounces.

The ammonium comes in the form of a heavy liquid and has a disagreeable odor. It should be mixed with clear water. As it decomposes on contact with the atmosphere, it should be prepared freshly each day.

CLEARING SOLUTION.

Water, ... 8 ounces.
Nitric Acid, C. P., ... 1 dram.
Mix together in a bottle.

STRIPPING SOLUTIONS.

It will generally be better to purchase these preparations, particularly the first, as making it involves considerable skill. Rubber stripping solution is made by putting into a wide mouthed bottle a quantity of perfectly pure and unvulcanized rubber cut into small bits, and covering the same with benzole. After a few hours the rubber will swell into a jelly-like mass. More benzole must now be added, under constant shaking, until a liquid the consistency of molasses is formed. This will take several days, the period varying greatly, according to the purity and freshness of the rubber. When of the proper consistency it should be filtered through cheese cloth. It is then ready for use. Do not expose to the sun, as this has a tendency to thin the solution permanently. It gradually loses its tenacity, and no more should be prepared than will last six months. If too thin, it may be thickened by the addition of rubber or the eva- poration of the benzole. If too thick, benzole must be added. This solution dries rapidly, but as benzole is quite expensive, many prefer to dissolve the rubber in benzine, which dries much slower. There are many grades of this article on the market. That which is usually sold under that name is not fit for the purpose.

Stripping collodion (No. 2) is made by dissolving thirty grains of gun cotton in three ounces of alcohol, and adding three ounces of ether and one dram of castor oil. The gun cotton need not be of as good quality as for negatives. The ether should be concentrated sulphuric, and 95 per cent. alcohol will do very well. Allow the mixture to settle until it is perfectly clear, when it is ready for use. The rubber stripping solution will have somewhat the color of muddy water, the collodion, almost white, but both when applied to a glass should give a perfectly clear and transparent coating. If only slightly tinted yellow, green or red, the printing quality of the negative will be seriously impaired, and better materials must be secured.

CHAPTER IV.

MANIPULATION.

As the glass is used repeatedly, it will pay best to purchase that of a superior quality. Chance's twenty-six ounce English glass is the best, it being freer of flaws and straighter than any other. Next in quality to this is genuine French negative glass. American glass, though considerably cheaper, is so full of flaws that its use is not economical. The sizes generally used are eight by ten, ten by twelve, eleven by fourteen and fourteen by seventeen inches. Even for small work it will pay to make a plate eight by ten inches. Before using the glass the rough edges should be removed with a file, otherwise there is danger of cutting the fingers. It is of the utmost importance that the glass be perfectly clean. Plates which have been used or new plates may be laid in a tub or stone jar kept beneath the sink containing a can of concentrated lye dissolved in two gallons of water. A few hours before they are to be used, take them out and wash thoroughly under the tap. When all traces of lye have been removed, place the plate in another jar containing one gallon of water and eight ounces of nitric acid. After several hours, remove the plate and again wash thoroughly, first beneath the tap and afterwards with distilled water, and then polish clean with Joseph paper. Many prefer to hold the glass in a wooden vise while so doing. Lastly, put it on a negative rack, in a clean place, to dry. Avoid touching the plate with the fingers after it is clean. The slightest particle of dirt or dust will make a faulty negative. A good test for cleanliness is to breathe on the plate. If the moisture disappears evenly the plate is clean, but if it clings to any spot it must again be polished with a paper or chamois skin. Obstinate grease spots may sometimes be removed with alcohol. The use of polishing material, such as rouge or chalk, should be avoided, as it will adhere to the edges and eventually disorder the bath. To avoid trouble from the film leaving the glass, dip a small wad of cotton in rubber stripping solution and run it around the edges of the glass on the side to be collodionized so as to cover a strip one-fourth of an inch wide. Be careful to get none on the rest of the glass, and make the coating as thin as possible. Unless the glass is perfectly straight, select the concave side. A number of plates may be prepared in this manner, as they will keep for any length of time. Some photographers prefer to use albumen in place of the rubber solution. It is made by beating up the white of an egg, adding twenty ounces of water and again beating. When the solution has settled and has been filtered, it may be applied with a wad of cotton as above directed, or with a soft brush at the side of which is attached a stick as a guide. To avoid the mistake of collodionizing the wrong side of the glass, the edges of which have not been treated, pieces should be placed to face the same way in the rack. In case there is any doubt, breathe upon the surface, when the difference between the clear and coated glass will at once be made apparent.

If you can get some collodion photographer to show you how to manipulate the plate you will save a good deal of trouble, otherwise pour a few ounces of collodion into the collodion vial, dust off a piece of glass carefully with a fine camel hair brush, hold it with the thumb and two first fingers by the corner C, as shown in Fig. 10, and, going to the dark room door so that you will have good light, pour a quantity of collodion near the center of the plate, covering about two-thirds of it ; incline the glass so that the pool will run to the corner A, clear to the

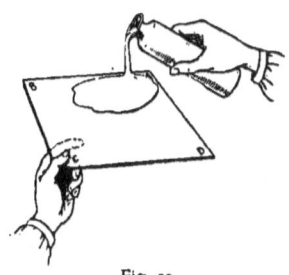

Fig. 10.

edge but not over it, then incline it so that it will run towards B, C, and finally D. Do not breathe upon the plate while so doing. If the plate is a large one the center may be supported on a bottle from the neck of which a clean cork projects. Supporting with the fingers is likely to warm the plate and cause spots at these places in the finished negative. Hold the plate so that the corner D is slightly lower, and pour the surplus back into another wide-mouthed bottle reserved for this purpose, as in Fig. 11. These drippings may afterwards be filtered

back into the pouring vial. While draining, the plate
should be held at an angle of fifteen degrees, which should
gradually be increased until the greater
portion has drained off. As it begins
to set, the plate must be rocked with
a gentle motion so that the coating will
be as uniform as possible. This is
done by moving the hand which holds
the bottle, and also the plate in the
neck of the draining bottle, so that the
point A moves towards E. If this is not
correctly done the plate will have waves
on the coating, and will be much thicker

Fig. 11.

in one portion than in another. The bottles are now stoppered and
put aside. Many photographers do not drain all the surplus
into a bottle, but wipe off the ridge which forms at the bottom
edge with their fingers. As the plate dries it should gradually
be made to assume a perpendicular position, the rocking being
continued until the collodion sets and becomes the consistency
of soft wax, which may be noticed from its appearance. It can
also be determined by pressing the thumb against the corner of
the plate where the collodion was poured off. If an impression
is retained, and the collodion shows no tendency to leave the
plate, it has set to the proper degree. Always wipe the mouth
of the vial before and after using. The lid of the bath holder
box is now raised, the dipper pulled out and the edge of the
plate A B laid on the projections at the bottom of the dipper,
which is then lowered at a moderate speed. Unless this is done
steadily without stoppages, there will be streaks across the finished negative. It is best that the plate holder should not allow
the plate to come within an inch of the bottom, otherwise the
sediment which accumulates in the bath may produce pin holes
on the plate. A peg can be placed in the handle of the dipper
so that it will rest against the top of the holder and prevent the
plate from going in too far. Now close the lid of the bath holder
and the dark room door.

It is presumed that the camera is in position on the swing
or stand, with the lens in the center of the lens board, and that
the copy has been pinned up somewhere near the middle of the
copy board. It is also to be supposed that the copy is good—

clear black lines against a dull white surface. Do not attempt
to make a very large or difficult job at the beginning. If you
are also to furnish copy you will do well to consult "Copy for
Photo-engraving." In fastening on the copy, see that the tacks
do not throw shadows which interfere with the drawing. Now
put your eyes close to the ground glass and cover your head
with a piece of cloth so as to exclude all light, shift the camera
and bellows until the image upon the ground glass is the size
you wish the cut. Do not attempt to reduce it much on the
first trial. Finally, the screw or lever at the back of the camera
must be moved gently until, when examined with the focusing
glass, the image is sharp, clear and evenly lighted. Focus half
way between the center and edge of the drawing. A good
focusing glass is highly desirable. Some experts dispense with
it, but this is not advisable. While focusing, put the diaphragm
having the largest hole, in the lens. When the image is perfectly clear and distinct, take out the large diaphragm and substitute a smaller one. This will make the image sharper by
excluding the outside rays, and will necessarily make the exposure longer. For a small cut which occupies the center of
the field, the second or third size stop may be used. Now put
the leather cap on the lens, return to the dark room and close
the door. Turn back the cover of the bath holder, raise the
dipper gently, and when the plate projects sufficiently, grasp it
by one of its corners and allow the surplus fluid to drain back
into the bath. It generally takes four or five minutes to sensitize a plate. If, on taking it out, it appears of an even, creamy
color, and the surface smooth and glassy, it may be removed.
If, however, it is streaky, and the solution looks as though it
was running over a greasy surface, it must be carefully replaced
in the bath and moved about in an easy circular motion. The
plate should be allowed to remain in the bath at least a minute
after the greasy appearance has left it. When it presents a
satisfactory appearance, drain by leaning it on the shelf with
the upper edge against the wall, the lower edge resting against
a pad of blotting paper. The edge which was lowest while
flowing on the collodion, and at the top when in the bath, must
be at the top while draining. Allow the plate to rest for a short
time on the blotting paper. The period will vary with the size
of the plate, two minutes being about right for an eight by ten.

While it is draining, wipe the back dry with another piece of blotter. It is then ready to be placed in the plate holder. If this is of the old type, you can readily see into which kit it will fit. If it is a Bonanza or Benster holder, the trough must be raised so that the plate will be in the center of the holder. Now place the plate so that the sensitized side is towards the front, then close and fasten the door. In all these operations be careful not to turn the plate so that the silver solution will flow back over it. Make sure that the slide is in its place and carry it in an upright position to the camera. Remove the ground glass, lay it in a safe place, and put the holder in the position before occupied by it. Now put the camera cloth over the holder and pull out the slide steadily, letting the cloth cover the aperture. If this starts the camera swinging, steady it before removing the cap from the lens. The length of exposure will depend upon the light, make of lens, and size of diaphragm, varying from three to twenty minutes. The advice of a photographer will be of much assistance to you at this point. If you have no one to help you, better make a number of negatives with the same light, giving various exposures and noting the results, or first pull the slide only half way out, so that part of the plate will be exposed longer than the rest. After exposure, place the cap on the lens and shove in the slide squarely. If one corner is pushed in first, it may open the shutter and allow the light to shine on the plate. Carry the holder into the dark room, holding in the same position as when it was exposed. Set it in its place on the shelf, close the dark room door and windows, and remove the plate from the holder. Hold it by the same corner as when flowing on the collodion, but keep the edge which was at the top of the holder and bath slightly above the others, otherwise the small amount of surplus silver solution which may have accumulated while the plate was at rest may flow back on the plate and stain the image. Previous to entering the dark room, see that the developer is in good condition and ready for use. A glass beaker makes a good pourer. Hold it with the left hand, its mouth close to the edge opposite that by which the plate is held, and with a quick motion pour out the solution so that it will flow over the plate in one even wave. If this is done hesitatingly the development will be uneven. Care should, however, be taken that no more developer runs

over the edge than can be avoided, otherwise silver will be carried away and the resulting plate be weak. Now hold the plate
in a horizontal position, and rock gently from side to side so as
to keep the developer constantly moving. The image will
gradually appear. If the exposure was correctly timed it will
take about six or eight seconds, the whites or lightest parts of
the copy first making their appearance. When you can see
the finest details distinctly, the development must be stopped.
If not carried far enough, the finer lines will not print clearly,
and the background will not be sufficiently opaque. If overdeveloped, the lines will become fogged or filled up. If you
have not allowed sufficient time for exposure, the effect will be
the same as if under-developed, except that in addition some of
the finer details will be entirely lost, and it will take longer to
develop the image. If over-exposed, the image will flash up as
soon as the developer is poured upon it, and on intensifying the
fine lines will be filled. It sometimes happens that the plate
has been under-exposed. This may be noticed by the length
of time taken for development, as well as the weakness of the
image. Should the plate have been over-exposed, adding a
little more alcohol to the developer will retard its working and
improve the plate. As the bath acquires alcohol from the collodion the developer will refuse to flow evenly on the plate, the
film repelling it as though it were greasy. Adding a very little
alcohol to the developer will overcome this difficulty. A better
way is to simmer down the bath in a porcelain dish until it has
been reduced to half its volume, and then add distilled water
until it registers forty degrees on the hydrometer.

The plate is now ready for fixing. On account of its poisonous nature, many prefer to keep this solution in a bath holder,
lowering the plate into it as when sensitizing. Generally it is
poured off and on the plate until the yellow color disappears.
After each day's work, a small piece of cyanide of potash may
be added to retain its proper strength. If not strong enough,
the lines will not clear properly, and are liable to fill up when
intensifying. If too strong, the negative will not be sufficiently
intense and will clean the plate instantly instead of gradually.
After fixing, the plate is again washed off under the tap until
the last trace of cyanide is removed. It is then placed in a tray
which contains the No. 1 intensifier, and allowed to remain

until the film turns white. If the plate has been properly exposed it will take about ten or fifteen minutes to do this. Never intensify in the dark room; a bench near the sink is the best place. This operation will not require watching. When the plate has bleached white it is removed, the surplus solution being allowed to drip back into the tray. It is again thoroughly washed. This takes considerable time, as the bichloride of mercury does not easily dissolve in water. Ten minutes under the tap is none too long, and if more time can be allowed it will do no harm. Now pour on the No. 2 intensifier in an even wave, as directed with the developer. This will immediately turn the film an intense black. Leave it on until the color has penetrated through the glass, then wash it off at once. The clear spaces will now have a slightly yellowish or greenish appearance. To remove this, pour the clearing solution on and off until the lines are perfectly transparent, pouring the surplus solution back into the bottle. Should the resulting negative be imperfect in any respect, some one of the manipulations has been faultily performed, or the chemicals and apparatus were not in perfect condition. These faults will be treated in the next chapter. After the plate has again been washed it is placed in the rack to dry. If the drawing was left-handed, the negative may be at once used for the printing on zinc. As generally made, the cut would be reversed, i. e., print would read from right to left. To correct this the film must be stripped from the glass and fastened to another piece upside down, that is, the side coated with stripping solution next the glass. When entirely dry, rubber stripping solution is poured upon it so as to cover such portions of the plate as are intended to be used. Pour the surplus back into the bottle and place the glass on a level shelf to dry, where no dust will get at it. When it no longer feels tacky, collodion stripping solution is poured on it in the same manner. During both operations the plate should be rocked to prevent streaks. It will take but a few minutes for this to dry thoroughly. Now cut around the picture with a penknife so as to leave one-fourth inch margin around the design. Be careful to cut clear through to the glass, and lay the plate in a tray containing barely enough clean water to cover it well. In a few moments the film will commence to part from the glass without any assistance. In the meantime, carefully clean a piece of glass for stripping. Thin plate-glass one-fourth of an inch in thickness, or twenty-six ounce English glass, should be used for this purpose. Place one edge in the tray containing the negative, then lifting the film, turn it upside down and lay it in the center of the glass. If a number of negatives of a similar class of work have been prepared, they may be attached to the same piece of glass. With the aid of the finger tips, or preferably a rubber squeegee, smooth the film to the surface of the stripping glass, being careful to avoid wrinkles or folds. If undue force is exercised, you are liable to tear the film or draw it out of shape. The squeegee consists of a strip of very soft rubber six or eight inches long fastened to a wooden handle. A weather strip can be made to answer, but being comparatively rough it is liable to injure the film. If the stripping collodion was made according to the formula given, and the manipulations were carefully performed, the film will adhere to the glass smoothly and closely. Should it show a tendency to curl away, the albumen solution used for coating the edge of the plate, as directed in the preceding part of the chapter, should be poured upon the surface of the glass, and the film squeegeed upon it. Generally a failure in this direction may be attributed to insufficient cleaning of glass. The film must be allowed to dry, when it is ready for printing. Films may be stripped from the glass and kept between the leaves of a clean book. If care is taken to prevent folds or wrinkles they will keep in this condition for years, and can be printed at convenience. Transparent celluloid may with advantage be substituted for the stripping glass, its flexibility insuring contact without danger of breakage.

CHAPTER V.

DEFECTIVE NEGATIVES AND THEIR CAUSES.

The beginner generally experiences his greatest difficulty with photographing. Bath and collodion seldom act well when new. Even after everything is in perfect running order, failures often result without apparent reason. If you cannot obtain the advice and assistance of a professional, be sure you have located the fault before you attempt to correct it, otherwise you will only increase the damage. Never dust out the dark room, but wipe it out occasionally with a damp cloth. It is well to sprinkle the floor to prevent dust from being raised by walking upon it.

The greatest trouble is the so called "fog," which makes opaque or only translucent such parts of the negative as should be perfectly clear and transparent. The fumes of ammonia and hydrosulphuret of ammonia will always cause fog. These chemicals, and preparations containing them, should never be allowed within the dark room. Escaping sewer gas, coal gas, and the gases produced by the combustion of coal oil and gas, will sometimes cause fog, but can usually be located and avoided with little trouble. If, on holding the finished negative to the light, the lines are not free from every trace of color or mist, test the bath with blue litmus paper. If the paper remains unchanged, add nitric acid C. P., under constant stirring, until the paper has changed a decided red. After a short rest the bath will be ready for use. Do not make the mistake of adding too much acid, otherwise the trouble will only be increased. A newly prepared bath which fogs slightly will often give perfect negatives after a night's rest. If the bath gives an acid reaction, collodionize and sensitize a plate and proceed to develop and fix it without exposure in the camera. Unless the plate is perfectly clear, the fog was probably caused by white light entering the dark room, or by the collodion. First test for light, carefully looking over every portion of the dark room to see that no stray rays are admitted. Holes or cracks must be covered with paper. If your light comes from a window, cover it with another sheet of heavy orange paper or glass. If from a lamp, substitute a small candle and try again. If the plate still fogs, it is probably due to the collodion being alkaline. Add a few drops tincture of iodine, or enough old collodion to give it the color of Maderia wine. If this does not remove the fog the developer is probably too strong. This can be detected by the image on an exposed plate making its appearance too rapidly. Dilute it with a mixture of acetic acid No. 8, two ounces; distilled water, eight ounces. It sometimes happens that during development an irridescent coating of silver floats upon the surface of the developer in constantly changing spots. This must be washed off, otherwise it will settle on the collodion and make a foggy plate. The cause is obscure, being probably a lack of harmony in the preparations. When water is supplied from a wooden tank it often happens that it becomes contaminated, in which case its use will cause fog. If in doubt, try distilled water in its place. If the unexposed plate develops without trace of color, the cause must be sought outside the dark room. Prepare a fresh plate, place it in the camera, draw out the slide (leaving the cap on the lens), expose for five minutes, then take it back to the dark room and develop. If the plate has fog, the cause is a defective camera or plate holder,

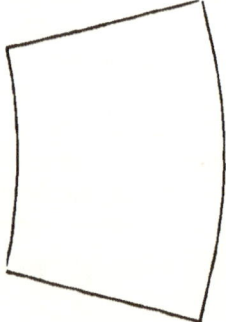

admitting light. This can easily be located and remedied. Generally it is not evenly distributed, but in the form of streaks. If this plate also is clear, and if the copy consists of black lines upon a white background, the cause is probably over-exposure. This is by far the most frequent cause of fog. It can usually be detected by the development being much more rapid than normal. Try another negative with shorter exposure. If, however, this plate also is clear, the cause is reflected light entering the lens. Cut a piece of card-board into the shape of Fig. 12, stain the inside black and fasten it to the lens, as in Fig. 13, moving it around so as to cut off all light. It would be safer to put the guard

Fig. 12.

completely around the lens, but this will make it awkward for putting on and removing the cap. The above directions will locate the reason of the fog, except such as is caused by under or over-development, too strong fixing solution, and allowing the glass to remain too long in the No. 2 intensifier. Judgment as to the length of development can only be acquired from experience. The

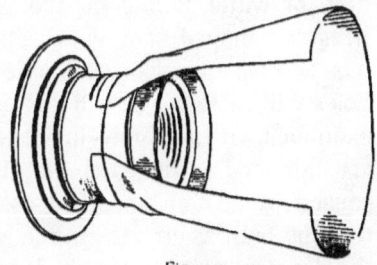

Fig. 13.

other causes can be located by watching the progress of the plate.

Should the film vary much in intensity, and the corners be lighter than the center, it was caused by the use of too large a diaphragm. If any part of the plate is less intense than the other, and always the same part, it is caused by uneven lighting of the copy. If the daylight enters from the window, or if you are using electric light, this is almost sure to be the case at the beginning. Reflectors made of white paper and mounted on suitable stands must be placed so as to equalize the light, and the camera stand must be moved according to circumstances. Use a small diaphragm while trying the light. Careful experiment alone will determine the size and angle of the reflectors. If the inequalities vary in position, they are probably caused by uneven films of collodion. Indistinct negatives are often caused by lack of care in focusing, or by imperfect apparatus in which the ground glass and sensitized plate do not occupy the same position. Spots and stains often make their appearance, sometimes without apparent cause. Above all, keep your hands and apparatus perfectly clean. If you allow dust to accumulate in the dark room, it will make small spots or "pin holes" in your negatives. If dust accumulates in the camera, it may be set in motion by the current of air started by putting the plate holder in position. Should it settle on the plate while you are collodionizing it, or should the collodion be unsettled, the spots will have small tails termed "comets" by photographers. The remedy is to clean the dark room and filter or settle the collodion. Setting the plate holder down with force or driving the slide in with a jerk will cause the un-

combined silver solution to splash on the surface of the collodion, and result in spots ending on one side with a point. A
drop of water falling on the plate while flowing will give an
irregular shaped spot which appears to be rough. If the bath
has become over-iodized from constant dipping, numerous pin
holes will be found distributed over the entire surface. When
examined with a magnifying glass they will be found to be small
crystals, and without tails, in this respect differing from those
caused by dust or unsettled collodion. The remedy is to correct the bath as directed in the last part of this chapter. Should
the developer be too strong, it may make pin holes very much
resembling those last described. When the cyanide of potash
in the fixing solution has absorbed as much silver as it can, it
also will deposit fine crystals on the plate, much like those last
mentioned, but as these do not make their appearance until fixing, the cause can easily be located and remedied by using new
fixing solution. Small, brown spots of a star-like character are
caused by not washing off all the developer before fixing. If
the plate be covered with irregular marks somewhat the shape
of oyster shells, or whitish insensitive spots, it is caused by exposing the plate so long that parts have dried out. The remedy
is to secure more light or a better lens, so that you will not require so much exposure. In very warm weather, placing a
sheet of wet blotter behind the plate and in contact with it
while exposing in the camera will help, by retarding evaporation. New baths sometimes produce marks in the shape of
oyster shells, but after a few negatives have been made they
will disappear. If the developer be too strong, or if it be not
flowed on with a perfectly even wave, it will cause streaks and
stripes at once apparent. If thrown on with force, it is likely
to make a spot at the point of contact, with lines radiating from
it. Should the collodion be too strongly salted, a scum will
form on the surface of the bath which will adhere to the plate
and cause zigzag lines to appear all over its surface. It can be
cured by adding plain collodion to the vial, but if the plate be
rapidly withdrawn from the bath the scum is not so liable to
adhere. An air bubble in the collodion will make a narrow, curved
mark. Such plates should not be sensitized, as the negative
will surely be defective. Should the film be mottled and have
a clouded appearance, the collodion is too thick or the coating

has been improperly done. If the negative shows minute but regular marks somewhat like the cells in a honey-comb, it is caused by poor quality of gun cotton or an excess of ether. The remedy is obvious. Should the plate be covered with fine ridges running in the same direction, it is caused by the collodion not being rocked properly until set. Should these ridges appear high, curved and whitish after sensitizing the plate, they were caused by the breath or a draft striking the plate while collo-dionizing. Thick collodion and improper flowing or rocking will also cause crapy lines like curtains. If the plate be not lowered into the bath with a regular motion, each stoppage will be apparent in the finished negative by a white line across the plate where its course was arrested. If lowered too quickly, it will cause streaks in the direction of the dipping. If lowered before the collodion has set sufficiently, it will be spotted. This will be more noticeable at the corner D than at any other. If the film be allowed to dry too long before developing, the upper part of the plate will have insensitive spots of a bluish color. If removed from the bath too soon irregular greasy marks in the shape of rivulets will be produced. Should a plate dipped into a new bath be of a bluish cast instead of a rich creamy color, iodize it more by putting in another collodionized plate over night, as before directed. Should the temperature of the dark room fall below seventy degrees, it may cause the same fault. Should the glass be improperly cleaned, the film is liable to tear and metallic silver will form between the glass and film. Tearing may be caused by an excess of alcohol in the collodion making it rotten, in which case the plate will have a rough appearance.

As has been noted throughout this and the preceding chapters, the bath is the chief source of trouble, yet with ordinary care one will last for years with but little correction. It has been estimated that a square foot of collodion will take about 30 grains nitrate of silver from the bath. An amount equal to that taken out should be replaced every night in the form of concentrated solution, so that the hydrometer will register the proper degree. With the utmost care organic matter will eventually so accumulate as to cause fog, pin holes, spots and streaks. Boil the bath down to about half its volume in a porcelain evaporating dish to expel the alcohol, as before directed. Neutralize the acid by adding concentrated water ammonia until red litmus paper is turned blue by it, and expose in a large, white glass bottle to the rays of the sun for at least two or three days. In the meantime the duplicate bath should be used. Before the second one commences to fail, the bath which has been sunning should be diluted with water so as to register forty degrees on the hydrometer. It can then be filtered back into the bath holder and acidulated with nitric acid C. P., when it will work as well as new. Another way is to place the bath in a bottle and add a solution of one dram permanganate of potash in six ounces distilled water, a few drops at a time under constant stirring, until the bath remains pinkish. It is then well shaken and set in the sun until clear. This procedure is excellent for a bath which is only slightly disordered. When in very bad shape, it is recommended to pour the bath into a large evaporating dish and apply heat. The water will gradually evaporate, leaving grayish crusts on the bottom and sides of the dish. Carefully increase the heat until these crusts melt into a clear, oily liquid free from bubbles. Allow this liquid nitrate of silver to cool and set, when it can be redissolved and the solution made into a new bath. From constant use the bath will also acquire an excess of iodide of silver, which will cause the crystaline pin holes before alluded to. Take a large evaporating dish, and for every gallon of the bath put one quart of distilled water into it. Pour the bath into this in a small stream. Do not reverse the order of pouring. Iodide of silver will be thrown down in the form of a white precipitate. After filtering, the bath is to be steamed and sunned, as before directed, to remove the alcohol and organic impurities. New baths as sold by dealers must be acidified, and also iodized before using.

CHAPTER VI.

THE PRINT ON ZINC.

It is difficult to obtain zinc of a uniformly good quality. The only satisfactory test is actual use. Ordinary sheet zinc will not answer, as it contains too much lead, iron, sulphur and carbon. Procure it from a reliable dealer. Cheap zinc is dear at any price. If, after etching with a five per cent. solution of nitric acid, the zinc shows streaks on both sides, like the grain of wood, it has been improperly rolled. Small holes or black lumps in relief show the presence of impurities. If a few small scraps are dissolved in nitric acid C. P., and if on addition of sulphuric acid C. P. a strong white precipitate is formed, too much lead is contained to fit it for etching. The side which appears smoothest is not always the best. Make a test of a sample cut from one sheet, and observing the characteristics of the roll, further tests are not necessary with the same lot. For printing purposes thick sheets are most desirable, but the expense of the metal and the extra trouble in polishing and handling have so decreased the thickness that one-sixteenth inch is the standard generally adopted. This will weigh in the neighborhood of two and one-fourth pounds to the square foot. It is seldom rolled exactly to gauge, but these figures are close enough for an estimate. One-fourteenth inch is often used for better grades of work. Zinc generally comes in sheets sixteen by thirty-six inches, and is cut into smaller pieces according to size of work. One-third of a sheet (twelve by sixteen inches) is the size generally selected, but the etcher should always have on hand polished pieces of every size from five by six inches to one-half sheet. For cutting the zinc, select a table from thirty to thirty-two inches in height. On the front edge nail a strip of hard wood or brass one-fourth of an inch thick so that the end will be eighteen inches from the end of the table. This strip is designated by A in Fig. 14. Nail the corresponding strip B parallel with it and seventeen inches back of the front. Lay

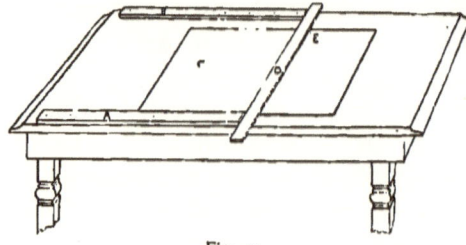

Fig. 14.

the sheet of zinc C between the strips, and the straight edge D upon it and against the ends of the strips. A piece of long primer or pica rule will make a good straight-edge. Grasp the zinc hook, Fig. 15, in the right hand and, holding down the straight-edge and the zinc with the left, set its point at E, about half an inch from the further edge of the zinc. Now draw it towards you, guiding it by the straight-edge with a light pressure, so as to cut out a triangular strip of metal. Repeat this operation several times until an appreciable groove has been cut in the zinc, then remove the straight-edge and, applying the pressure of the left hand to the end above the point, follow the groove already formed. When about two-thirds through, the zinc must be given a half turn, so that the half inch between E and the outside edge can be cut. When the sheet has been

Fig. 15.

cut three-fourths through it may be removed to the edge of the table, when the parts can easily be separated by bending two or three times.

Some etchers use a saw, but this will raise a burr and is liable to bend the sheet. The edges are now to be rounded with a file so that there will be no danger of cutting the fingers while handling. If the sheet is not perfectly flat, lay it on a straightening block (an old press bed will answer nicely) and straighten it with a mallet and planer. A hard wood block two by three by two inches can be substituted for the latter. For polishing, a tray should be mounted on legs, as illustrated in

Fig. 16, so as to slant at an angle of about 30 degrees. Twenty by twenty-four inches is a good size. The bottom edge should be about thirty inches from the floor, so that the polisher can bring his weight into play. Preferably, it is lined with zinc or made water proof in some other way. On the bottom lay a

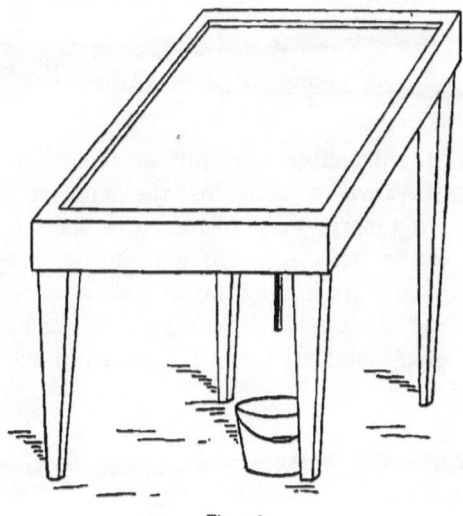

Fig. 16.

pad of three or four thicknesses of canton flannel, and fasten it with tacks so that it will not move. This will prevent the zinc from slipping under pressure. The bottom right hand corner should be provided with a hole, and be somewhat lower than the other corners, so that all the water will run to it. Fasten a piece of heavy packing twine in this hole so that the drippings will run along the twine into the bucket below the bench. Lay the zinc upon the pad, file a piece of pumice stone so that it will present a flat surface one or two inches square, dip it in the water and rub vigorously in one direction only—to and from you. Always lay the zinc so that the lines of rubbing will conform with the direction in which the zinc was rolled. Select pumice stone of the finest quality and remove bits which break from the lump, otherwise you are liable to make deep scratches which will be difficult to remove. At first the oxide or grease on the outside of the zinc will repel the water, but in a few moments the pumice stone will take hold over the entire surface. When the scale has been thoroughly removed, which can be easily noticed by the zinc assuming a bright, metallic appearance, wash it off by pouring water upon it. If there are any serious imperfections caused by rolling, set it aside. If, however, there are only small holes and streaks here and there, wipe the plate dry. Now, holding it in the left hand, grasp the callipers (Fig. 17) in the right, pass the upper point immediately around

Fig. 17.

the outlines of the defective spot, but not in contact with the zinc, pressing the lower point against the back of the plate so that it will leave a mark. On turning the sheet upside down the location of the defective spot will be at once apparent. When all the spots are located, lay the sheet upside down on the straightening block and with a punch and hammer, or preferably a smasher hammer, Fig. 18, tap within the outlines of

Fig. 18.

the mark so as to bulge the zinc slightly on the other side. When all the spots have been beaten up, return to the polishing bench and rub again with pumice stone, removing the lumps. This will cause the holes to disappear unless they are very deep, in which case the operation must be repeated. Next take a piece of Scotch stone about the size of your fist and file a small flat surface upon it. Polish in the same direction as before, until the scratches made by the pumice stone have been removed. Be careful to clean the zinc and pad thoroughly, and to use fresh water in polishing, as a small bit of pumice stone may make a serious scratch when the work is nearly finished. Do not use more water than sufficient to allow easy movement of the Scotch stone. Wash the surface with clean water from time to time. Should more holes make their appearance, locate them with the callipers and beat out as before directed. When the surface appears smooth it may be placed in an etching bath composed of sixteen ounces of water and one ounce of nitric acid 38°, and etched from five to ten minutes, the surface being meanwhile brushed with an etching brush. Provided the zinc is of a good quality, this will smooth it, and at the same time remove the top layer of zinc, which is generally not as good as that below it. Remove the plate from the bath, wash thoroughly and again polish with Scotch stone. Many photo-engravers do not etch at all, but proceed directly from the Scotch stone to the final polish. Others use a zinc scraper, Fig. 19, laying the plate on a level surface and applying pressure with both hands in the same manner in which the zinc hook is used, and scraping in parallel lines until the outer layer is removed. This is a most excellent method, and when followed, the rubbing with pumice and the subsequent etch may both be omitted. When dull, the edges of the scraper can be sharpened by rubbing them on a piece of emery cloth stretched over a block of wood. Ordinary charcoal will not answer for polishing zinc, as it makes deep scratches. That sold for this purpose by photo-engraving supply houses should be obtained. It usually comes in pieces about three by five by one and one-half inches. Cut each block length-wise into two pieces. This will make the block of convenient size. Dip it into water and polish carefully in the same direction as before, until the fine scratches made by the Scotch stone have been entirely ground away. Use the end of the block first, and the grain side for finishing. Some etchers now grind into fine powder the finest willow charcoal, such as used by artists, mix it into a paste with olive oil, and give a final polish,

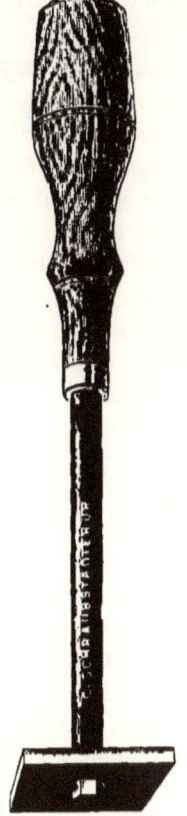

Fig. 19.

pressing it on with a wooden block. Others buff the zinc and polish with rouge. Large establishments use leather buffs, coated with emery powder of various grades, to remove the outer coating; and give a final polish with whiting or rouge in the same manner. The fineness of the work depends greatly upon the finish of the surface, and this work should not be entrusted to a boy, as it requires considerable strength, skill and experience. Experimenters will do well to purchase their zinc ready polished, and many larger establishments pursue this course. Etchers differ as to the desirability of graining the p..ate before sensitizing, some maintaining that it spoils the surface, while others claim this operation should never be omitted for fine work. Make a bath of one quart of water, one dram of nitric acid and one ounce of saturated solution of alum, and place it in a rubber tray. Select a piece of zinc a little larger than the job you wish to engrave, and lay it face uppermost in this solution. In four or five minutes it will become gray and acquire a very fine tooth or grain. Wash it carefully and, while wet, take it into the dark room. Never allow the plate to dry before pouring on the sensitizing solution. The water should flow over evenly. Should it be repelled by any part of the plate, it is caused by grease, which must be washed off before the albumen solution is poured on. Avoid touching the surface of the plate with the fingers. Another way to clean the plate is to pour a small quantity of aqua ammonia upon it and rub over the surface with a tuft of absorbant cotton. To prepare the sensitizing solution, take the white of an egg, and after removing the germ, beat to a froth. Then add eighteen grains bichromate of ammonia dissolved in eight ounces of distilled water, and beat again; some etchers add a few drops of conc. water ammonia. Now filter through a wad of absorbent cotton lightly pressed into the neck of a funnel. It is best to support the funnel on a funnel stand, and filter into a wide mouthed bottle. Do not allow the solution to drip into the bottle, but let it run down the sides, otherwise it will be full of froth and air bubbles. The amount of albumen contained in an egg varies with its size, but the above proportions are close enough for practical use. Where fresh eggs are not obtainable, dry egg albumen (half an ounce for the quantity above specified) may be used, but it is more expensive and less satisfactory. After a few hours the rest of the solution is ready for use, but as it rapidly deteriorates, something easily discernable by the odor, it should be freshly prepared every few days. A larger proportion of bichromate of ammonia shortens the time of exposure, but limits the period of exposure and heightens the chance of having the print under or over-exposed.

While the plate is still wet take it to dark room No. 2, hold it by the lower left hand corner and pour the sensitizing solution on the upper right hand corner so that it will flow entirely over the plate. Pour on a little more than is necessary to cover the plate, allowing the surplus to run to waste. Repeat the pouring several times, so that the solution will be full strength, undiluted by the water which was on the plate. If poured too rapidly, or if the mouth of the bottle is held too far from the plate, air bubbles will surely result. See that the solution is fresh, perfectly clear, and free from bubbles or froth. Should any bubbles be formed by accident, pour on more solution until they are washed away, otherwise when the print is developed a white spot will result. Slant the plate at an angle of ten or fifteen degrees, so that the surplus solution will drain towards

Fig. 20.

one end, and hold it over an oil or gas stove to dry. Do not use a lamp, as you are liable to smut the plate and break the chimney. Be careful that the plate always slants in the same direction, so that the surplus sensitizer does not run back over the dried part. As it forms at the lower edge remove it with a bit of blotting paper. Avoid heating the plate too much, or the albumen will be cooked and the coating rendered insensitive to light. For this reason it is best to hold the plate in your hands, as any heat that can be borne by the fingers is safe. The plate should be allowed to dry gradually from the upper end. In the meantime the printing frame must be prepared. Many engravers use a modification of the photographer's silver printing frame with heavy cross bars containing screws instead of springs. The kind illustrated in Figs. 20 and 21 is preferable, inasmuch as the strain can be much more evenly distributed, and the front will not be pushed out by repeated pressure. The glass should be perfectly flat, smooth and transparent. For small frames, three-quarters of an inch thick is amply sufficient. For larger ones, one inch may be used. Take the frame apart and carefully clean the plate glass. Replace it in the frame, and should it fit loosely, fasten it with wooden wedges. Lay the frame upside down, as in the illustrations, place the stripping

Fig. 21

glass to which the film is attached and the sensitized zinc face to face, and lay them glass side down on the center of the print-ing frame glass. Before so doing carefully dust both sides with a fine camel hair duster, as the least grain of foreign matter will break the negative or plate glass when pressure is applied to the screws. Lay the backing board upon the zinc and slide the screw plate in above it. Be careful not to move the zinc after it has been placed in contact with the negative. Now turn the screws until you feel resistance. Do not bring any one home, but gradually tighten them until they offer a mod-erate amount of resistance. Beginners are apt to press too hard,

cracking the negative or even the heavy glass. Do not tighten
the screws which are beyond the confines of the zinc. Now
expose the plate to the light. This can best be done by resting
the frame on a stand constructed for the purpose, and which
can be set at various angles. If sunlight is chosen, a shelf
should be constructed to extend from the window frame. In
direct sunlight the exposure will vary from two to eight minutes;
in diffused or electric light, from six to thirty minutes. Only
experience will enable the operator to time the print correctly.
Beginners had best divide the plate into four parts. After a
short exposure cover one-quarter with some opaque material,
then an additional quarter, and finally the third quarter. By
keeping track of the time each space was exposed and noting
the results upon development, the proper period can easily be
ascertained.

In the meantime, in the dark room preparations should
have been made for rolling up. For this an old lithographer's
tint roller which has been carefully handled is the best. It
should be perfectly smooth and free from lumps and indentations. Such rollers can seldom be purchased, and are almost
invaluable. Lithographers' rollers are made by fixing several
layers of flannel cloth to a wooden core and covering the outside with calf skin, the core being allowed to extend so as to
form handles. For smooth rollers the hair side is on the outside. If carefully made the seam is imperceptible to the touch,
and almost invisible. From use the skin gradually becomes
saturated with ink and the surface glazed. If carefully handled,
not only will the seam become invisible but the surface will be
free from holes and lumps, and the roller will acquire an elasticity which it is impossible to impart by any other means. If
you cannot obtain an old roller in good condition, you can purchase one prepared or prepare it yourself. Put a little castor oil
upon the inkslab and roll up the unprepared roller until the
leather and flannel are saturated with it. Avoid an excess: you
must not be able to squeeze out oil by pressing on it. Let the
roller rest for a few hours, then pour a little lithographers' middle varnish (No. 2) upon the slab, and roll up until the leather
will absorb no more. Do not put more varnish on the stone
until the first lot is entirely absorbed. Constantly change the
direction of rolling, so that the varnish will be evenly dis-

tributed. When the roller will absorb no more, lay it aside for three or four hours, then repeat the operation. Do not leave any varnish on the outside of the roller, but roll up until it is entirely absorbed. This operation must be repeated once or twice a day for two or three weeks. When the roller will not take up any more varnish, scrape off the excess lengthwise with a blunt knife (the back of an old case knife will answer very nicely), being careful not to cut the leather. Lay it aside for four or five days and again roll up with heavy varnish (No. 3). After removing the excess of varnish the roller is ready for use. Middle varnish must be perfectly clear and transparent, and when a small portion is lifted from the mass it must run out into threads two or three inches long. When rubbed between the fingers it must make a distinct crackling noise. Heavy varnish is almost as thick as gum, and but a small portion should be spread at a time. In cold weather the slab may be warmed. During the operation of rolling up, and afterwards, both slab and roller must be preserved from the dust. It is best to make a low wooden box to cover the slab, and on it rest a wooden support which will hold up the handles of the roller and prevent its surface from touching the slab. Still a better way for preserving the roller is to purchase a tin roller cover made for the purpose. Handle covers made of heavy leather will greatly assist in rolling up. In place of a lithographic roller, many etchers use one of composition. It should be cast of large diameter and be perfectly smooth. As usually prepared for printers' use, they are too soft. Very little suction is required, but the surface should be straight from end to end. Better have a roller cast of hard composition. An ordinary one, on drying out to the proper hardness, generally shrinks so unevenly that it rests on the ends, and the middle does not touch the slab without undue pressure. Rubber rollers are sometimes used for the purpose, but as they are much more expensive than those of composition, they are not recommended. Ink made for the purpose should be purchased. Some grades of lithographers' transfer ink will answer, but often it contains too much tallow, and the developed image will not have enough strength to hold the etching powder or resist the acid. As good ink can be purchased at a reasonable price, and the beginner cannot make it properly without expensive apparatus, the formula will not be given. For the sake of convenience, this ink will be referred to as etching ink No. 1. Make sure that the roller is perfectly clean. If it has acquired any dirt from rolling up, scrape it off with a dull knife or rub with a rag dipped in turpentine. When thin ink is used for rolling up, it will not hold the etching powder sufficiently to resist the acid. As the thick ink is difficult to distribute, take a small quantity of it, place it on a slab and rub it with the ink knife so as to cover as much space as possible. At the side of the slab have a bottle of rectified turpentine, through the cork of which a small hole has been bored. Sprinkle a little of this over the ink and roll up until it is distributed smoothly over the slab and the roller. The least speck of dirt or undistributed ink may play havoc with the print. If the proper amount of ink has been used the slab will still be visible through it. As the rolling up proceeds the turpentine will evaporate, and more must be added until the distribution is perfect, but the plate should not be rolled up until the turpentine has almost all evaporated. Lay a piece of zinc with the exposed side upwards upon the slab and roll briskly until the plate is coated evenly. Turn the zinc from time to time so that the direction of rolling will be changed. If properly applied, the coating will be of a perfectly even shade, and so thin that the yellowish color of the bichromatized zinc can be plainly discerned through it. Beginners usually make this coating too thick. The plate is now taken from the dark room and laid face upwards in a shallow rubber tray, and enough clean, cool water is added to barely cover its surface. Allow it to remain for about five minutes, or until the water has penetrated the ink, then take a ·pinch of clean absorbent cotton, and rub it against the surface with an easy circular motion. Do not apply too much pressure, otherwise you will smudge the print. Commence on the margin, working towards the center. If the exposure was timed correctly the ink can be removed with little difficulty, and the engraving will appear in the form of black lines against a bright background. Should any part of the image be hard to develop, let it alone while you are rubbing the balance and come back to it afterwards. Do not rub longer than is necessary to bring out the clear image. If the plate has been over-exposed it will be difficult to remove the ink from the white spaces, requiring so much pressure that the lines will be smudged or obliterated. If under-exposed the image will rub off with the rest of the ink. The addition of a few drops of ammonia or saturated solution of bichromate of ammonia to the tray will often aid in the development of a plate which has been only slightly over-exposed. Should part of the plate develop and the balance fail to do so, it was probably caused by an uneven negative, or uneven distribution of the sensitizing solution caused by not flowing it as above directed. Heating the plate so as to cook the albumen will have the same effect, as will also imperfect union between the

Fig 2.3

zinc and the negative, caused by insufficient pressure on the screws or inequalities in the surface of the zinc or stripping glass. These defects can generally be located with little trouble. Should the lines be heavier than those in the negative, it is probably caused by the use of too much ink or undue pressure in development.

Wash the plate thoroughly in running water, blot off the water with a damp cloth and heat over a gas stove to a degree not hoter than the hand can comfortably bear. Lay the plate face upwards on the retoucher's table, take a little of the No. 1 etching ink, place it on a saucer and, thinning it with rectified turpentine, paint the borders within a quarter of an inch of the outlines of the cut, using camel hair brushes of various sizes. If the plate is to be finished by routing, or with the jig saw, paint the large white spaces in the body of the cut also, as this will save acid. Fig. 22 shows a proof of an engraving as painted in, and Fig. 23, the same cut after routing. Now place the zinc beneath the bridge, as illustrated in Fig. 24, and examine the print with a strong magnifying glass. If any lines are missing they must be painted in with No. 1 etching ink thinned with turpentine, applied with fine artists' camel hair brushes, of which there should be several. Should

Fig. 23.

the lines be too wide, or should there be any black spots, they must be scraped away. Lithographers' needles, the points of

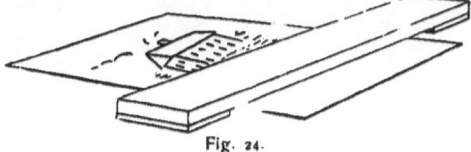

Fig. 24.

which are ground to various shapes, are best adapted to this purpose. The plate is now ready for powdering up, as directed in the next chapter.

PRINTING WITHOUT A FRAME.

Another method of making the print dispenses entirely with the frame. Numerous experimenters have succeeded in doing this, but the following, originated by Mr. Chas. Chetham in 1884, is by far the best. The advantages are: All danger of breaking either the stripping glasses or printing frame glass is avoided; it is easier to handle the plate than the heavy printing frame; where the zinc surface is not perfectly plane, the contact is better; the exposure is shorter; and the size of the zinc is not limited to that of the printing frame, as any number of films may be attached to a sheet and printed at the same time.

Both stripping solutions should be applied more thickly than is necessary when stripping glasses are used, so that the film will be heavier. It is sometimes necessary to add a little more castor oil to the stripping collodion than directed in the formula given in the last chapter, but this can be arrived at by trial. Strip the film as if for mounting on glass and dry it between blotters.

Coat the zinc in the usual manner with albumen sensitizing solution, and when it is dry pour a few drops of castor oil upon it, distributing it evenly with a clean composition roller. Lay the film upon the surface, commencing with one end and gradually lowering the rest as when fastening it to the stripping glass, and smooth it down with the finger tips. Air bubbles may be dispelled by piercing their centers with a fine needle. After exposure the plate is rubbed over lightly with a wad of absorbent cotton. The small amount of oil left upon the plate does no harm, and is really a benefit, as it assists the distribution when rolling up. For fine work, such as half tone, always use the printing frame. Beginners had best use it for coarse jobs as well, until they thoroughly master the other branches of the business.

CHAPTER VII.

' POWDERING AND ETCHING.

Dragon's blood is almost universally used for powdering the plate. It is a resinous gum, the exudation of several tropical trees. There are so many varieties of the pure gum, and there is so much adulteration that it should be purchased only from a photo-engraver's supply house. The best is of a deep red color, ground to an impalpable powder. It makes an excellent resistance against acids and is not liable to stick to the spaces between the lines. The only objection against it is its tendency to make the surface rough when melted, and its extreme brittleness. With proper manipulation these faults will give little trouble, and for the finest work they can be corrected by the addition of other ingredients. As these will vary, both as to quantity and kind, according to the qualities of the dragon's blood, it will pay far better to purchase than to experiment yourself. At least one pound of powder should be placed at the bottom of the powdering box. This is made of wood, about three inches in depth and several inches larger than the largest plate which it is intended to etch. In one end about an inch from the top is a cross strip. A hinged cover is thrown over it when not in use, so as to prevent dust from being mixed with the etching powder. Lay the retouched plate in the box, and with the flat powdering brush (one of fitch hair, and two and one-half inches wide, is best) heap a quantity of powder upon it. With the same brush distribute the powder thoroughly, allowing time for the ink to absorb as much as possible. Brush away the surplus powder with the same brush, then take a clean, heavy, flat camel hair brush two and one-half inches wide, used for this purpose only, and thoroughly brush again. Do not apply enough pressure to injure the lines. When the drawing is of a reddish brown color against a perfectly clean background of polished metal, it is ready for melting. For heat-

ing the plate, a covered oven with several rows of burners will
be found most satisfactory. One similar in construction to a
gas griddle, but having wires instead of a solid slab over the
burners, is recommended. For small work but one or two rows
need be lighted. Beginners can use an ordinary Bunsen burner,
moving the plate so as to distribute the heat. For holding

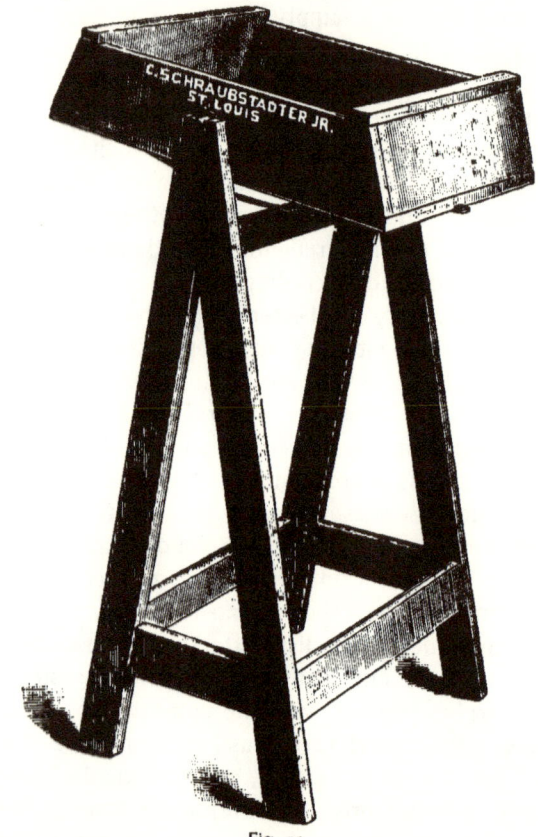

Fig. 25.

the plate during the melting on, a pair of wide nosed pliers will
be found most satisfactory. Hold the plate by one of its edges
and lay it on the wires. As soon as the powder melts and com-
bines with the ink, which is at once noticeable by its becoming
a bright, deep brown instead of the dull red, remove it from the
oven and lay it on the stone or metal slab. This should be
perfectly flat and be placed at the side of the oven. Should
the heat be continued too long the lines will become heavier,

the coating brittle and the zinc warped and twisted. Paint the back and edges of the plate with asphaltum varnish to prevent the acid from attacking the zinc in these parts. Heat the plate slightly to expel the turpentine from the varnish. When cool, it will be ready for etching.

The form of etching tub shown in Fig. 25 is most desirable. For ordinary work twenty by twenty-four inches is large enough. It should be acid proof and of well seasoned lumber. Some etchers use chemically pure nitric acid for the first etch, but the majority take the commercial grade, 38 degrees. Pour about one quart of water into the tub and add three quarters of an ounce acid. Rock the tub several times so as to mix well, then lay the plate in the center. Rock slowly so that the acid will run over the plate in even waves. In a short time the surface will become covered with a grayish deposit. This is removed by gently brushing with a camel hair or bristle brush used for this purpose only. The rocking need not be interrupted for brushing, neither should the brushing be continuous. Ordinary brushes set in glue will last but a short time, the acid rapidly destroying them. Rubber bound brushes sold for the purpose are the best, but those bound in tin can be made to answer by giving them several coats of asphaltum. Watch the zinc carefully, examining it from time to time under the retouching glass. Should any of the finer lines show signs of giving way, or should the zinc appear to show through the coating, the plate must be taken out of the tub, thoroughly washed, and the defective parts touched up, or the entire plate gummed, inked, dried and re-powdered, as directed in the next chapter. From time to time the plate should be given a quarter turn, so as to change the direction of the flow. The depth of the first etch will vary according to the class of the work. In crayon or fine line work the relief must not be more than the thickness of writing paper. For ordinary work the etching may be continued until the relief is that of a thin card-board. This will usually take from eight to ten minutes, and will be apparent by a bright rim around the lines. The thumb nail is usually applied as a test. Should the shoulder have progressed enough to engage the nail the etching must be stopped. With a very little experience the beginner can judge when the proper relief has been attained. When it is judged that the first etch has proceeded far enough,

take the plate from the tub and wash it thoroughly. Remove
the water by blotting off with a damp rag and then warm over
the oven. Now examine the plate carefully. Should any of
the lines be weak or the coating wholly removed they must be
touched up with a fine camel hair brush dipped in a mixture of
No. 1 etching ink and turpentine. If used thinner than the
consistency of cream, the ink will not be strong enough to hold
the powder or resist the acid. As it is very difficult to make
fine lines with such heavy ink, great care must be exercised at
this point, otherwise the lines will be too heavy in the finished
cut. Place the plate back into the powdering box and, covering it thoroughly with powder, rest it against the rail as before
directed. Hold the plate by the lower left hand corner, resting
the top against the strip in the powdering box, and brush in
lines parallel with the top and bottom, from right to left only,
lifting the brush on the return stroke. When the powder has
been removed from the surface of the plate, use the softer brush
with the same motion. When all the powder has been brushed
out of the white spaces, bring the plate to the oven and heat
as before, just sufficiently to melt the powder. Place it on the
slab, and when it has cooled grasp it by the lower right hand
corner and, resting the left edge against the rail, brush the
powder from the top to the bottom of the plate, again taking
the precaution to lift the brush on the return trip. Repeat the
melting and cooling, then put it back into the powdering box.
This time hold it by the upper right hand corner with the bottom edge resting against the rail and brush the powder from right
to left. Melt on the powder and repeat the operation, holding
the plate by the upper left hand corner, resting the right edge
on the rail, and brushing from bottom to top of the design.
Heat again, when the shoulder of the first etch will be found
thoroughly covered with melted etching powder. Always brush
against the plate, not away from it, otherwise you will dislodge
the powder from the crevices. While cooling for the last time,
add a little acid to the etching tub and rock so as to distribute
it. As the first etch has taken out a quantity, varying with
the amount of zinc dissolved, the tongue is the best standard.
Add sufficient to make it taste the strength of vinegar—from
one to two ounces. The second etch should be continued about
five or ten minutes, but the acid being stronger, the amount of

relief obtained will be greater. No standard can be given. The operator must use his judgment. At the beginning he had best err in making it too short than too long. The beginner may clean a portion of zinc at the edge where there is no design, so that he can make the thumb nail test before alluded to. Remove the plate and examine it carefully. If the job is a fine one, some portions will by this time have sufficient relief. Should the powdering fail to fill the counters, such parts must be painted over with the mixture of etching ink No. 1 and turpentine, otherwise the lines will be undercut or lost. The plate is then to be powdered and melted on four times exactly as before, when it is ready for the third etch. The quantity of acid and duration of the etch must again be left to the judgment of the etcher. Usually about the same amount as in the second etch is taken. Should the progress be too slow, a little more can be added from time to time as the etch progresses. It should always be borne in mind that too little will do no further harm than prolong the work, while too much will inevitably spoil the cut. If the work covers a plate fully, i. e., if the lines are close together, three etches will be sufficient. Very open work, such as diagrams, etc., will require as many as six or eight etches, the same precautions being taken as before. Unless perfectly straight, the plate is liable to float when a wave of acid strikes it. This is particularly true of small ones. It can be avoided by bending the plate slightly so that the back is concave, by rocking a little slower, holding the plate down with the fingers, or by fastening it to the box with a thumb tack. Nitric acid, even in the diluted state, will turn the skin and finger nails yellow. Even with the utmost care the etcher cannot altogether do away with this, but the greater part can be avoided by covering the hand. Rubber gloves are awkward, but the finger tips sold for the purpose will not seriously inconvenience him. From constant handling with pliers while hot, the asphaltum on the back of the plate will be worn off in places, so that the acid will attack it. Small holes, particularly on the edges, will do the plate no harm. Black spots of greater or less extent in the white spaces are generally caused by insufficient brushing or dusting. If they are small and appear after the second powdering, they need cause no alarm, as the strong acid of the second etch will

remove them. If, however, they are large, they must be carefully scraped off before etching. Should the zinc be of a poor
quality, so that it has projections and holes, it will cause the
same trouble. The only remedy is to scrape them off whenever they appear. Should any of the lines be lost, particularly
the finer and isolated ones, the fault probably lies in using too
strong acid, continuing the etch for too long a period, or heating the plate so much as to burn the coating. Other causes
are, brushing the powder too long, or away from instead of
against the plate, and ink or etching powder which will not
resist the acid. These faults, though much more apparent in
the finer lines, will also be noticeable in the coarser ones.
Irregularities at the bottom of the plate are generally caused
by poor zinc or insufficient and uneven brushing during the
etch.

Lay the plate on the etcher's oven and heat it sufficiently
to melt the coating. Take it to the sink and pour a little ordinary turpentine upon it. While still hot, brush rapidly until
the coating is dissolved away. It can then be given a final cleaning with lye or benzine, and polished dry with hot sawdust.
The sawdust should not be allowed to enter the sink, otherwise

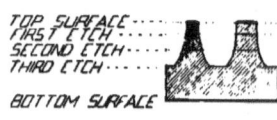

Fig. 26.

it will choke the drain. If the etching
has been properly done, both as re-
gards time and strength of acid, and
if the proper amount of powder was
allowed to remain upon it, the cross
section of two lines strongly magnified would appear somewhat
like Fig. 26, or like Fig. 27, each shoulder recording the limits
of an etch. In all probability, however, it will appear more
like Fig. 28. Should any of the lines be badly undercut, like
Fig. 29, so that the base is little wider than the top, it will be

Fig. 27.

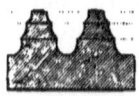

Fig. 28.

Fig. 29.

impossible to save the cut: it had best be thrown away and a
new one made. Should it appear like Fig. 28, take the plate
into the dark room No. 2 and spread a little No. 2 etching ink
upon the slab. This is stiffer and less greasy than the No. 1.

Carefully distribute, and roll it up with the addition of a little turpentine, but put a little more on the roller and slab than before directed. The No. 1 etching ink will answer, but is not quite as good. See that the plate is perfectly clean, warm it slightly and lay it on the slab. Roll over very lightly, so as not to ink up the blank spaces or the sides of the lines. Allow it to cool, then dust powder upon it. Melt it on, let it cool, dust again, and repeat the operation once or twice more, or until the ink will absorb no more powder. In heating up, be careful not to bring the plate to too high a temperature, otherwise the mixture will run too far down the sides. If properly done, only the top of the lines and part of the first shoulder will be covered. Now place the plate in the etching tub again, with fresh acid no stronger than that employed for the first etch. Examine it from time to time with a magnifying glass, and if the steps are not sufficiently reduced before there is danger of undercutting the lines, remove the plate and repeat the entire operation of inking and dusting, using more ink, or heat so that the coating will run down further on the sides of the lines. Clean the plate again, and if found right, clean the back as well, when it is ready for the router. Beginners are apt to leave too much powder on the plate when powdering, so that a cross section of the lines will appear like Fig. 30 when cleaned off for the first time. This is not nearly so serious a fault as if the lines were under-etched, since it can be cured

Fig. 10.

by rolling and powdering, as above directed, although in this case it may take several additional finishing etches. Large establishments run their etching tubs by power, using a separate countershaft for each tub, connecting with the main shaft in the finishing room. If properly balanced one horse-power is enough for many tubs.

ETCHING ON COPPER.

For the finer class of half-tone work, many etchers prefer copper. It should be polished and prepared in the same manner as zinc, but the weak acid used for the last named material would have scarcely any effect upon it. Unless the coating is unusually strong, concentrated acid would destroy it. For this reason a saturated solution of perchloride of iron is generally employed for the first etch, the plate being laid in a tray or suspended in a bath for ten or fifteen minutes. Unlike acid, the saturated solution of this salt will not attack the metal as much as one which has been diluted with water. Should even the concentrated liquid act too strongly, it must be reduced by allowing it to work upon a piece of scrap copper. After the first etch, wash off the plate under the tap, using a soft brush. It is then returned to the bath, the operations of etching and washing being repeated until the requisite relief is obtained. Nitric acid, two ounces to the quart, may be used for etching, but though faster is liable to undercut the fine dots.

CHAPTER VIII.

GUMMING UP.

Another method of protecting the sides of the lines is that of gumming and rolling up. The slab should be smooth, preferably of marble. A lithographic roller must be used for this purpose: one of composition will not answer. One with rough outside finish is best adapted to this purpose. They are generally termed "black," to distinguish them from the smooth or tint rollers, and should be prepared for use exactly in the same manner as directed in Chapter VI. Etching ink No. 1 can be made to answer, but one containing no fat, but instead, a mixture of wax and resin, will give better results. To distinguish this from the rolling up ink, it will be called No. 2. Back of the slab, have three shallow cups of glass or porcelain. Procure a fine velvet sponge of such size that when wet it will be a little smaller than the fist. Beat it out thoroughly and leave it over night in a mixture of one part hydrochloric acid and thirty parts water. This will remove the last trace of lime. Wash thoroughly, so as to remove all the acid. Put one ounce gum arabic in a wide-mouthed bottle and add about four ounces water. Stir it occasionally, and at the end of two or three days the gum will be thoroughly dissolved, forming a liquid of a syrupy consistency. Should any part remain insoluble in cold water, but simply swelled, the gum is adulterated. Strain the gum through a piece of muslin, and to every one hundred parts solution add three parts phosphoric acid. Stir thoroughly, and should it contain any impurities, filter again. Pour a little of this in the first cup, into the second place the clean sponge, and into the third, pure water. After the first etch, dip the sponge into the gum solution and rub lightly over the plate until it is coated with an even layer of gum about the thickness of writing paper. The coating must be perfectly smooth, without streaks or bubbles. The gum must now be dried. This can be hastened by fanning: do not subject it to heat. Take a little of the No. 2 etching ink and spread it on the surface of the slab with the ink knife. Add a little rectified turpentine and distribute it thoroughly. Lumps, however small, will make spots in the plate. The coating should be considerably heavier than for developing; about as thick as is used when proofing. Do not use more turpentine than necessary. When evenly distributed, squeeze the gum which is left in the sponge back into its cup, and dip the sponge into the cup containing water. Squeeze the excess of water out, and rub lightly over the zinc so as to remove the coating of gum from the surface of the lines, being careful not to rub so hard as to remove it from the white spaces. When the turpentine has evaporated, roll over the wet plate, pressing evenly and very lightly. At first the ink will not take readily, but with continued rolling the lines will be covered with a smooth, even coating. Should the ink stick to the white spaces, remove it by rubbing gently with the sponge which now contains a very diluted solution of gum arabic. Should the roller become wet from the plate, wipe with a clean rag and roll it out on the slab. When evenly coated, take the plate to the sink and wash it under a rose tap, rubbing very lightly with the sponge until all the gum is removed from the surface. Do not rub hard, otherwise you will smear the ink. When thoroughly clean, blot off the surplus moisture with a damp, clean rag, and dry with very gentle heat or a fan. Now take the plate to the powdering box and dust thoroughly until the ink will absorb no more. Be careful not to apply too much pressure, otherwise the lines will spread. Heat the plate sufficiently to make the powder combine with the ink. When cool, should the coating be tacky instead of firm, repeat the powdering and melting operations. If carefully performed, the shoulder made by the first etch will be completely covered and protected from the acid by the coating of ink and etching powder running down the sides. It may then be etched as before. After the second etch the same procedure may be followed, but a little more pressure should be applied when rolling up, so as to deposit some ink on the sides of the lines as well as on the surface. In the hands of a skillful workman the gumming and inking up will produce the finest results. It is, however, somewhat slower and much more difficult than powdering four times, therefore many establishments do not use it at all. Some gum up after the first etch only, using the powdering method for all subsequent etches, while others gum up only when the drawing appears weak. This last, however, seldom happens unless the job is very delicate, the ink or etching powder of a poor,quality, or so much heat is used in melting on as to make the coating brittle. Cleanliness is of the highest importance. The ink slab, sponges and cups should be covered when not in use, and be removed some distance from the powdering box. The slab should be cleaned often. Clean the roller every night by scraping lengthwise with the grain with a dull knife held slanting so as not to cut the leather, and keep it in a tin roller cover while not in use. If it is to be left unused for some time, rub its surface with tallow, but be careful to remove all grease by scraping before using again. The gum solution should be freshly prepared with acid every morning, and not more should be dissolved in water than will last two or three days. There is another method of gumming up, in which the ink is applied with a sponge instead of a roller. As this is more difficult, and, except in the hands of an expert, gives less satisfactory results, it will not be described.

Fig. 31.

CHAPTER IX.

ROUTING AND FINISHING.

In an establishment of any considerable size, power machinery is essential. The main shaft should be at least one and eleven-sixteenth inches in diameter, and be attached to the ceiling in a line about eight or ten feet behind the finishing machinery, by hangers of at least twelve-inch drop. Self-oiling hangers which require filling but once in three months are most economical. The speed of the shaft will vary, according to circumstances, from one hundred and fifty to two hundred revolutions per minute.

There is great difference of opinion as to what speed the spindle of the router should run. Some recommend as high as 15,000 revolutions per minute, but in practice it has been found that the speed of from six to ten thousand revolutions per minute is amply sufficient. In a router running at this last named speed, the spindle pulley being two inches in diameter, and the belt running six inches at each revolution, the latter will travel five thousand feet, or almost a mile, per minute. Such speed will soon tell on the belt and wearing parts of the machine, even when of the best material, and a higher rate will increase this wear in greater proportion than the additional speed. Fig. 31 shows one of improved construction. The machine should be placed in such position that a good light will be thrown on the work. Should a sheet of zinc be warped by over-heating during the etching operation, it must be straightened and then clamped firmly to the bed of the router. The form

Fig. 32.

of cutter shown in Fig. 32 is preferable. Most operators prefer to grind the tools so the back will present a view shown in Fig. 33. This increases the efficiency, enabling the workman to do much more work in the given

Fig. 33.

time, but does not make quite so smooth a finish as when the bottom edge is almost square. The cutter must

73

be tightly fastened into the spindle. Pressing the foot on the treadle will bring the cutter against the zinc, the depth of cut being regulated by adjustment of the screw on the head. It requires considerable experience to rout closely to the lines without occasionally cutting into them. The cutters preferred for general work are three-sixteenths and five-thirty-seconds of an inch in diameter. After finishing with one of these tools, many of the best photo-engravers remove it and substitute a smaller one, one-eighth or one-sixteenth of an inch in diameter, routing out such places as will not admit the larger tool.

Fig. 34.

Fig. 34 shows the fluted cutter generally employed for type metal and wood. Always keep the cutter in good condition, sharpening from the bottom edge only. Do not touch the side. If properly done the routing will leave ample relief in every part, and without any burs. Many photo-engravers give the final or finishing etch after the routing, so as to remove the sharp edges formed by the cutter and give the cut a smooth and even appearance. Foot power routers are impracticable. The high speed required for zinc, and the consequent exertion, will shake the operator so much that the work must be done very slowly, and fine work cannot be done at all. The beginner who cannot afford power machinery had best send his work to some electrotype foundry for routing and blocking, or etch it down to proper depth. Still another way is to purchase a light jig saw, not such as used by electrotypers, but the kind generally employed for fret work, carrying a saw about one-sixteenth of an inch in width, and saw completely around the cut, leaving only enough room for the tacks. Large spaces in the body of the engraving may be cut out in the same manner, by first making a hole with a hand drill for the insertion of the saw blade. Both of these procedures are, however, comparatively slow and unsatisfactory. After the plate has been routed it is taken to the circular saw and the edges trimmed away as much as possible, somewhat as shown by the dotted lines in Fig. 35. The speed of the saw will of course depend largely upon its diameter. For a seven to nine-inch saw, 3,000 revolutions per minute will be found about right. The same blade will not cut wood, metal or zinc equally well. The wood blade would dull and stick in zinc, and the zinc blade would heat and wedge fast in wood. The form known as hollow-

ground is much to be preferred, although for wood an ordinary saw with teeth properly set will do. Even here the hollow-ground blade is to be preferred, as it does not require so much skill to keep it in order. For wood, there should be three or four teeth to the inch; for type metal, five or six; for zinc, eight, and for copper, eleven. The shape of the teeth will differ slightly according to the material. It will pay to purchase the very best. The saw should be sharpened whenever dull with a three-square file (the ordinary saw file, having blunt

Fig. 35.

edges, will not do nearly so well), and occasionally trued by raising the table until the edge of the saw barely projects, and passing a small slip of oil or grindstone over the opening while the saw is revolving. Different blades may be put on the same saw mandrel, as required. A better way is to purchase separate frames, or one having two spindles, as illustrated in Fig. 36. Revolving the handle will make one saw descend and the other rise in its place. Almost all cuts are mounted on wood. Mahogany is preferable, but on account of its cost cherry and birch are generally chosen. It will vary in thickness according to the gauge of zinc, and should be perfectly flat and even. Unless there is sufficient work to warrant the purchase of a Daniel's planer, it is best to buy the wood planed to the correct thickness. Be sure that it is dry and thoroughly seasoned. Saw off a block about one-eighth of an inch larger than the engraving. Small mounting blocks are generally made in a single piece. When of considerable size, particularly when there is no certainty that the wood will not warp, the main piece is grooved like B, Fig. 37, and the side pieces A should be tongued so as to fit into the mortises. There are special machines made for this purpose, but the work can also be done on the routing machine, Fig. 34. Another way is shown in

Fig. 36.

Fig. 38. The main block has triangular grooves planed in the sides. Inasmuch as the end strips do not receive the

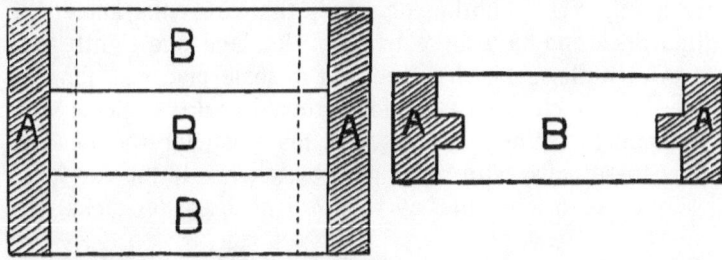

Fig. 37.

tacks, they may be made of hard wood, such as oak. When the blocks are very large, the center is often composed of several sections, like B, Fig. 37, spaces being left between adjoining pieces to prevent warping. Still another plan is to score the bottom of the cut with the saw, cutting

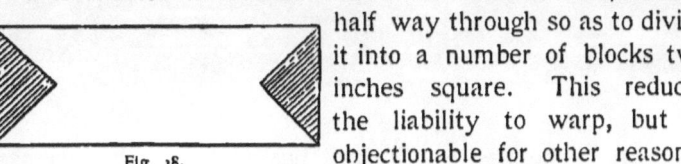

Fig. 38.

half way through so as to divide it into a number of blocks two inches square. This reduces the liability to warp, but is objectionable for other reasons. Remove the sharp corners from the zinc plate with the file, lay it on a piece of hard wood, and with a hammer and nail punch make small holes at frequent intervals, as illustrated by X in Fig. 35. With the file remove the burs formed at the bottom of the plate, and if the zinc has been bent, straighten it carefully. Rest the wood

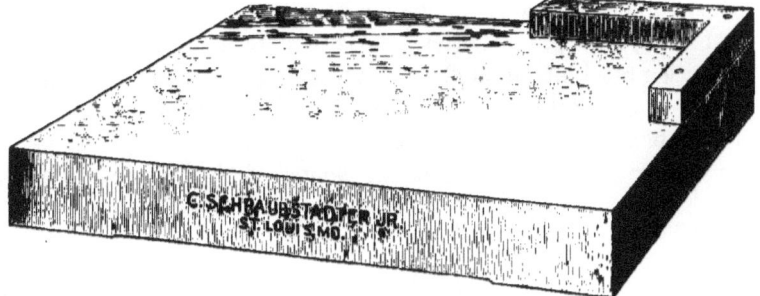

Fig. 39.

block on the finishing plate, Fig. 39, and lay the zinc upon it. Place it somewhere near its position, drive in a single tack, and then turn the zinc until the cut is square with the corner of the block, which rests against the squaring device of the finishing plate. Then fasten it down, when the other tacks may be driven in. For mounting on wood, the wire nails should be rather thick and have large heads. Half and five-eighth inch are the lengths generally used, but in some places as long as three-fourth inch are used. They should be driven home with a nail punch. Where the space is too small for the head of one of these nails, wire brads may be taken. If the cut be so closely covered with lines as to afford no space for tacks, the

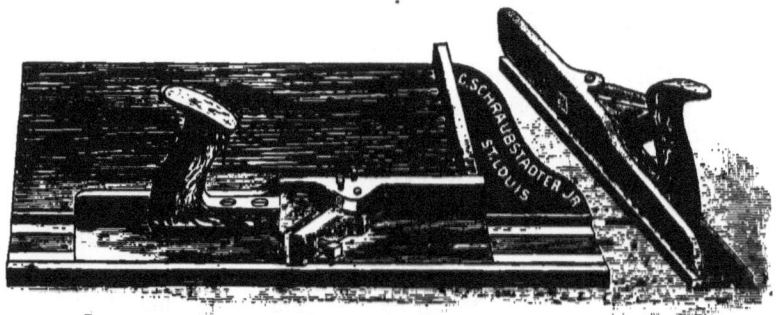

Fig. 40.

edge may be beveled in the shoot board, Fig. 40, by using a special beveling plane. It can be fastened to the block by driving the tacks diagonally into it, as in Fig. 41. This necessitates the use of a block slightly larger than the plate, and is objectionable for the

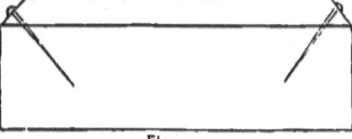

Fig. 41.

reason that the plate, not being held at the center, is liable to bow and warp. A better way is to bore holes through the mounting block about one or one and one-half inches apart, and about three-eighths of an inch in diameter. At one end they should be counter-sunk so that a cross section of a hole will be

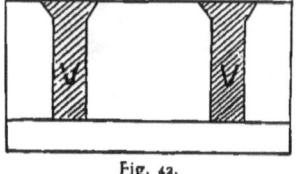

Fig. 42.

in the shape of V, Fig. 42. The zinc plate is then laid face downward, and the back polished with emery cloth. Lay the block above it with the counter-sunk end of the holes upward, and clamp them firmly together. In a small ladle, heat ordinary plumber's solder, and pour it into the holes so as to barely fill them. The heat will be sufficient to fasten the solder to the plate, and the counter-sink will attach it firmly to the block. It is best to put a very little resin or a drop of soldering liquid at the bottom of each hole. Care must be exercised not to make the solder too hot, otherwise each point of attachment will show on the face. The plate is now ready to be trimmed, which can best be

Fig. 43.

done in the machine shown in Fig. 43. Like the saw, the spindle should make about three thousand revolutions per minute. The cutters should be set so that they barely clear the table, and that the cutting edges of the knives are horizontal when half way through the block. The cutters used by electrotypers for metal, although they will not make as clean a cut as the grooved blades used for wood, are preferred, as the latter

are rapidly dulled by the zinc. When re-ground, care should
be exercised to keep the cutting edge the original slant, to set
them firmly into the head at the correct angle, and the proper
distance from the sliding table.   Tightening them into the head

Fig, 44.

may cause them to shift position so as to cut into the table. If
there is any appreciable space between them, the edge of the
wood will be broken down and rounded.   This is no serious
defect, but detracts from the appearance of the finished cut.
Some engravers avoid this by fastening a piece of electrotype
metal along the edge of the table with deeply counter-sunk

screws. When the cutters are sharpened, they are set so as to take a slight cut from this metal projection of the table, thus preventing the edges of the cut from being rounded. In operating the trimmer, the set screws are loosened and the gauge moved up so that a slight cut will be taken from the block. The set screw in the rear of the gauge is then tightened. Blocks are seldom sawed accurately, and always a little larger than necessary. If the cut is not perfectly square on the block a small piece of folded paper can be placed between one end of it and the gauge, so as to throw it over. The operator stands arms crossed before the machine, and with his right hand holds the block firmly against the corner of the gauge. After the first cut the left hand turns the gauge screw so as to push it forward and take another small cut. After squaring the first side the others are trimmed off close to the engraving. Where space is an object, the combined saw and trimmer, Fig. 44, can be substituted for the separate machines. New machinery should be carefully watched to see that bearings do not get hot, and as it wears, the bearings should be tightened up. Loose pulleys should be oiled at least once a day, and rapidly revolving spindles, three or four times. The belt which passes over the router spindle should be occasionally examined, and if it shows signs of giving out, be replaced with a new one. As it runs at a very high speed, it is liable to give the operator a severe blow should it give way when running.

The use of metal bases is confined almost exclusively to newspapers. For this purpose they should be exact column

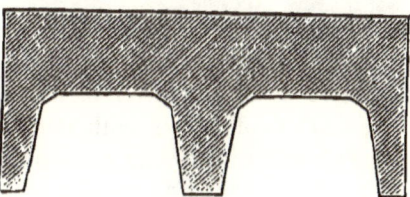

Fig. 45.

widths, regardless of the width of the cut, and consequently need not be trimmed on the sides. Solid metal bases will answer very well, but on account of their great weight are not generally used, except for half column cuts. Cored bases, Fig. 45 representing a cross section of one, are much easier to handle, and less expensive. Bases may be purchased of proper width and height, or may be cast in body molds made for the purpose, in which case they must be shaved to accurate height in the shaver, Fig. 46. The zinc should be fastened to

Fig. 46.

them with stout wire nails a quarter of an inch in length. Small establishments can cut blocks with miter box and saw, and square them with shoot-board and plane shown in Fig. 40.

The plates are now ready for the first proof. This need not be very carefully made. The cut, together with the proof, is then passed to the finisher, who examines it closely, and if not certain on any point, refers to the copy from which it is' made. For touching up, an eye glass, stand, and leather pad are highly desirable, but not essential. The gravers should be ground at a more obtuse angle than are wood engravers' tools,

otherwise the edge is liable to break off. There is some difference of opinion as to whether round or flat edge gravers are
best for this work. The majority of finishers prefer the latter,
as the bottom of the tool can be used to touch up the sides of
lines where the relief is not sufficiently sharp. Frequently
some of the lines will be too heavy, and spots occasioned by
defective manipulation will appear. These must be carefully
cut out. Zinc is a very difficult metal to engrave. It
is by no means infrequent that the lines at the edges
of a cut print heavy. The most approved method of
lightening them is to run over them with a roulette,
Fig. 47. This instrument consists of a brass handle,
in the middle of which may be held various corrugated
wheels having sharp teeth of different sizes. Held
between the thumb and fore-finger of each hand, it can
be guided with light pressure so as to dot the lines.
Fig. 48 shows a cut before being treated with the roulette, and Fig. 49 the same cut afterwards. The improvement can easily be seen. Many artists, however, object to the slightest change in the copy. After
being carefully retouched the cut is ready for final
proof. A Washington hand press is best for this purpose, but an army press can be made to answer.
Usually one of the former can be purchased second-
hand at a reasonable price. It will pay to give careful
attention to the proof, as it is by this that the customer
will form his opinion of your work. Clean the ink slab
very carefully and distribute a very small quantity of
ink with a good roller. Heavy coated paper is generally employed for this purpose, consequenly the ink,
though an intense black, should not be too thick. Distribute it carefully over the surface of the cut. Place

Fig. 47.

this in the center of the press, and around it, several old cuts
to act as bearers. If the cut is heavy in the center, and has
but few outrunning lines, a portion of the ink may be removed
from the latter with the tip of the finger or a light dabber.
Place the paper carefully upon the block, and above it, ten or
fifteen sheets of smooth heavy paper, lower the tympan and
roll the bed beneath the platen. Give a good light impression,
and if the proof is not perfect, try again until you have secured
as good results as are possible.

The thin zinc plates are extremely liable to warp, and where the lines are isolated they are in printing often driven into the

Fig. 48.　　　　　　　Fig. 49.

wooden block. Whenever the edition is a large one, an electrotype should be made and the original cut preserved.

CHAPTER X.

Printing with Asphaltum.

As has before been noted, asphaltum was one of the first substances to be used in photography. For the finer grades of work it is still largely used in place of the bichromatized albumen for printing on zinc. The greatest objection to be urged against it is the length of time required for exposure. Formerly this was several hours, but modern methods of extracting the less sensitive portions have reduced the time, so that it now requires much less time. The advantage is that unlike the albumen print, which is developed by rubbing off the surplus ink, there is no danger of spreading the lines in manipulation.

This substance is known as Egyptian asphaltum, Syrian asphaltum, and bitumen of Judea. It varies greatly in respect to sensitiveness. The best quality is of a deep brown color, approaching black, but the edges of the lumps where rubbed appear much lighter. When broken, the surface shows fine shell-like configurations. Samples which appear the same vary so greatly that it is advisable to purchase this material sensitized and prepared for use, from some photo-engravers' supply house. If you wish to make it yourself, procure asphaltum of the finest quality, break it into small lumps and place it in a large, wide-mouthed bottle. Pour in about four or five times its bulk of concentrated sulphuric ether, stir thoroughly and let it stand for a few hours, stirring it frequently until the ether has absorbed some of the asphaltum and is turned a deep brown color. This liquid must be poured off, more ether added, and, with occasional stirring, the bottle allowed to stand for a somewhat longer period. If the asphaltum is of a good quality, this fluid will be a great deal lighter in color than the first. It must be poured off and replaced with fresh, and this process continued until the ether though frequently stirred is but very lightly colored. It is then poured off, and the solid mass re-

maining at the bottom allowed to dry.   The fluid of the last
few washes may be preserved for the first washing of another
lot of asphaltum: the balance is of no value.   When entirely
free from ether, dissolve one ounce of the powdered residue in
fifteen ounces pure benzole.   Filter through cotton, filtering
paper or, preferably, chamois skin, into a yellow bottle.   All
these operations had best be carried on in dark room No. 2.
The solution is now ready for use. In some varieties of asphaltum the extraction of less sensitive parts by ether leaves the
residue so brittle that it will not adhere to the plate.   In such
cases a small quantity of oil of lavender or Venice turpentine,
previously boiled to expel the water, must be added to the benzole solution.

Polish the zinc and copper thoroughly.   Then take the
plate into the dark room and flow the coating of asphaltum over
it, as with collodion, taking care not to run over any part of
the surface more than once.   As the benzole evaporates quite
rapidly, it is difficult even for an expert to coat a plate evenly
in this manner.   A much better way is to purchase a whirler,
shown in Fig. 50.   After the plate has been cleaned, place it in

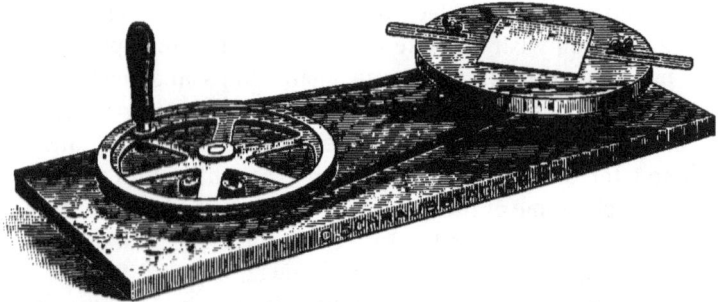

Fig. 50.

the center of the disc, clamping it down by the edges, as illustrated in the cut.   Now pour sufficient solution upon it to cover
two-thirds of the surface, then revolve the hand wheel as rapidly
as possible until the plate has dried.   This will take but a few
moments, and on removing it the plate will be covered with a
thin coating of a golden color.   Streaks or spots are generally
caused by the benzole containing a small amount of water.
After the solution is a few days old, plates may show minute
dark spots.   These are caused by decomposition of the solution.
The remedy is to filter it immediately before using.   The plate

may now be slightly warmed, so as to drive off all the benzole. It is then ready for printing. This must be done in the printing frame, and in the same manner as with albumen. The exposure will vary from fifteen minutes in direct sunlight to two or three hours in diffused light. It can only be ascertained by experience, and will vary with different samples of asphaltum, or the same lot treated differently. Pour rectified turpentine into a shallow porcelain or glass dish, to the depth of about one-fourth inch, and then lay the exposed plate into it. Rock the tray gently, when the print will gradually make its appearance. When the whites appear clear, remove the plate and plunge at once into the dish of water. Wash well under the tap and examine with a strong glass. If not sufficiently developed, blot off the water, replace in the tray, and continue as before. Should only part of the print be backward in development, rub lightly over the surface with a small piece of absorbent cotton dipped into the rectified turpentine. When completely developed, the entire plate will appear as if covered with a scum. Place it in a bath of benzine. This will remove the remaining turpentine and leave a clear sharp print. Wash off the benzine with water, blot off the surplus moisture and expose the plate to sunlight for ten or fifteen minutes. This will harden the asphaltum and turn it somewhat darker in color. It is then ready for etching as directed in the previous chapters. The first etch should be of comparatively weak acid, and should not be continued for a long period. Before the second etch the plate should be gummed up, as before directed. Should the image be weak, or should it fail to develop at all, the entire surface washing away, the print was under-exposed and another one must be made. If the plate develops with difficulty, or not at all, the trouble was over-exposure or, what is more probable, the negative was not sufficiently intense. In general, it is to be noted that over-exposure is not nearly so much to be feared as under-exposure.

CHAPTER XI.

H A L F - T O N E .

This is at once the most interesting and difficult engraving method. Not only are skill, attention and experience necessary, but the result will also depend largely upon the operator's artistic ability. In most instances the work will be portraits or landscapes with photographs for copy. These should present rich contrasts and be full of detail. A certain proportion of the copy is cut out by the screen, consequently the resulting plate will be weaker than the original. Pure whites cannot be obtained without sacrificing the details of the darker parts except by routing, and unless the copy presents rich contrasts the plate will look flat and uninteresting. Often the copy may be improved by touching it up with Chinese white, but this requires a skillful artist. Experience will soon teach you what copy to reject as unlikely to produce satisfactory results.

There are a number of methods of changing the tones into lines or stipples. Generally a modification of the Meisenbach process is used. In the original method an ordinary negative is first made. This is placed in contact with another sensitive (dry) plate and a dia-positive made from it. This dia-positive or transparency is placed in the front of an enlarging and reducing camera, Fig. 6, with the lens back of it. It is then focused on the ground glass. When the image is sharp and of the correct size the sensitized collodion plate is placed in the plate holder, and immediately before it, separated but a short distance, the screen plate, having fine lines ruled in one direction. The plate is then exposed. If it is desired to make a plate having the tones in the form of dots instead of lines the plate is exposed but for a short time, and taken to the dark room where the screen is given a quarter turn, the sensitive plate remaining in the same position. It is then given another exposure either the same length of time or a shorter period according to the result it is desired to achieve. If properly exposed this plate will have, instead of the delicate shadings of the original, dots and lines which give the same effect. The variation of this method which follows is much simpler, quicker and less expensive. While better detail and contrast are secured by using screen plates ruled in one direction only, and exposing twice, approximately the same results can be obtained by giving but one exposure behind a screen plate in which two series of lines cross each other, and better modulation of tones will be secured than by the double exposure. Screen plates are generally made on thin clear glass. The lines may be ruled through some opaque material made to adhere to one of the surfaces, or they may be etched beneath the surface and filled with some dark varnish. Such screens are the best, as they can be frequently cleaned. The great expense of their production and the liability to break or scratch the glass prevents their general adoption. Generally, photographic copies of such screens made on collodion dry plates are used, as, if well made they work almost as well as the original, and with careful handling will produce a great many good negatives. Dust or splashes of silver allowed to touch the prepared side will ruin them very quickly. As to the proportion of lines there is great difference of opinion. The closer they are together the nearer will the plate approach the softness of tone of the original copy, but the more difficult will it be to procure a perfect negative, make a good plate, and print it after it is finished. Except on coated paper, with the best ink and press work, the finest half-tone cut will have a most unsatisfactory appearance. It has been found that one hundred and twenty-five lines to the inch will produce dots which will not be obtrusive. If made finer than one hundred and thirty lines to the inch, the details will be better brought out, but the results are apt to be unsatisfactory, except with the most careful attention on the part of the pressman. Lines as coarse as one hundred and ten to the inch will be hardly apparent with such inspection as is given by the layman, and will produce better contrast than those closer together. Screens are sometimes made as coarse as eighty lines to the inch for rough printing, but the result is hardly satisfactory. As to the relative proportion of the black to the white lines on the screen, there is also difference of opinion. Many workers who produce excellent results prefer screens in which the white lines are twice as heavy as the black lines. The majority, however, prefer those in which the black lines are little lighter than the transparent portions. Some prefer screens in which the lines running in one direction are lighter or closer together than those which cross them, as in such cases the lighter parts of the middle tints change from crossed to single lines before breaking into the dots composing the lighter tones, instead of changing abruptly from cross lines to dots, as is the case when both sets of lines are equal. If the screen were placed in close contact with the sensitive plate, it can easily be understood that the result would be the cutting out of such portions of the plate as were covered by the opaque lines, while beneath the transparent portions would be reproduced such parts of the copy as were before them. If the screen were placed any considerable distance away, yet still between the plate and lens, the effect would be scarcely noticeable, as the light entering the lens would pass around the opaque portions of the screen. If, however, the screen is placed but a short distance before the plate, say one-sixteenth inch, the light will, where it is intense, work around those parts of the screen where the lines cross, as well as the portions between the junctions, breaking the tints into lines and dots in the finished cut. The distance between the screen plate and the negative depends largely on the relative proportions of the transparent and opaque portions of screen, as also on the lens aperture. The only other articles required besides those used for line work are the kits. These are small frames made of well seasoned hard wood which fit into the plate holder. In the corners of each frame are fitted small distance pieces made of coin silver so situated that when the kit is placed in the plate holder and the sensitive plate pressed against the silver corners it will occupy exactly the same position as if it were put directly into the plate holder. Separate kits having distance pieces one-sixty-fourth, one-thirty-second, three-sixty-fourths and one-sixteenth of an inch in thickness are to be provided. As the frame must be stiff enough to be rigid, the screen plate must be a size smaller than the full capacity of the camera. Thus a ten by twelve camera will admit a half-tone screen and sensitized plate but eight by ten, an eleven by fourteen, one which is ten by twelve. As the silver pieces cut off the corners, allowance must also be made for these.

The utmost care must be exercised in making the negative. The collodion should be made with the finest gun-cotton or cellodine. The alcohol and ether as well as the salts should be perfectly pure. It should be of the proper consistency and perfectly clear and free from foreign matter or hardened crusts. The silver bath should be in perfect working order. Select a kit with corners of moderate thickness, say three-sixty-fourths of an inch. Place the screen plate in it so that the ruled side will afterwards face the collodionized plate. Fasten it with the clips and then secure it in the plate holder. Use an ordinary copying camera shown in Fig. 5 and focus sharply on the copy. If this is one of the modern photographs having a very highly glazed surface, be careful to adjust the light in such manner that it will not be reflected from the surface, otherwise it will be impossible to secure a good negative. Make sure that the plate is properly drained and then place it in the kit so as to face the ruled plate. The spring in the back of the plate holder will keep it in place. Take it to the camera and expose a little longer than you would for an ordinary line negative. The exact time cannot be given, as it will vary with circumstances. Were the conditions exactly the same it would be possible to give directions which would enable the beginner to determine the proper distance and length of exposure, but as the apparatus, screens, chemicals, diaphragms, light and—more than any of these—the copies differ in every case, experience alone will enable him to get good results. With the most successful half-tone engravers it is largely a matter of instinct, yet often they make several negatives of a fine piece of work before they secure one which is satisfactory. Usually it takes from once and one-half to twice the exposure required for line work. In general it may be noted that if in the negative the black lines of the screen plate are too distinctly reproduced, so that there will be little contrast, the screen was too near the sensitive plate or the aperture of the lens was too small. If, on the contrary, the lines are not sufficiently distinct and the spaces between them are filled in not with black dots of varying size, but with deposits of silver of uniform extent, and varying in intensity, the screen was too far from the plate or the aperture of the lens was too large. When a good negative has been produced the printing plate may be made by etching or by the gelatine

processes afterwards described. Generally it is etched on zinc
or copper. Here also the utmost care must be exercised. The
plate must be polished and buffed until the surface is perfectly
flat and free from scratches and indentations. The print should
not be made from a film, the printing frame must be used.
Asphaltum is preferable as the development is not likely to
blur the lines.

The smallest defect in manipulation, a speck of dirt on the
screen plate, negative, or in the printing solution will result in a
black or white dot in the printing plate and unlike line work it
is almost always disastrous to touch up the print or the finished
block, the correction being almost certain to show. The print
should be somewhat stronger than the finished cut. Use very
dilute acid, not stronger than one-fourth of an ounce to a quart
of water. The duration of the etch must be prolonged until
sufficient relief is obtained without losing the finer dots which
will become somewhat lighter. Generally half an hour is
sufficient. During this time the plate must be closely watched
through a magnifying glass, and if the fine dots show signs of
giving way the etching must be stopped. Some etchers gum,
ink and powder up, making two etches, but generally the required depth is given by a single bite. Powdering four times
is impracticable for half-tone work. The plate is now ready to
be mounted in the usual manner. As has before been noted,
pure whites cannot be obtainted in half-tone without sacrificing
detail in the shadows. When desired, such portions of the
print on metal, before etching, must be cleaned with scrapers
of different shapes. Unless this is done by some one of considerable artistic skill the result is apt to be bad. If the original
has good contrast, pure whites will not be necessary to obtain
a satisfactory effect. The whites may also be removed by
graver and routing tool after the cut has been etched and
proved. In such case the edges are apt to be sharp and harsh.
They can be softened down after mounting by the judicious use
of the matting punch held securely against the corners and
tapped so as to lower them and ease the impression at these
points. The less retouching required, the better will be the
result. If properly made there will be a very few shadows of
pure black, semi-tones formed by black lines of varying thickness crossing each other, and in the lighter portions fading into

minute black dots. Occasionally even the very best negatives will be lacking in detail in the darker portions. This can be remedied by the judicious use of a pencil roulette, Fig. 51, making a few fine dots. Should any portion be too light it can be strengthened by the use of a steel burnisher, Fig. 52. This will make the printing plate lower at such points, but not enough to affect the printing. Small dots can be removed with a finely pointed graver, but if the screen is a good one and the plate properly made they will seldom appear. Small white spots are often present in the best cuts, but if dust is carefully excluded they will be so infrequent as to be un-noticed. Very often the cut can be improved by painting a border around it with a mixture of etching ink and turpentine. If the border is to consist of straight lines, this can be done with a ruler, the entire margin being covered before the plate is etched. If in the form of an oval or circle, a glass pattern is generally employed. If the cut has been etched, the margin is routed out so as to leave a black line surrounding the cut. This can be trimmed up either on the shoot-board or with a graver. Both zinc and copper

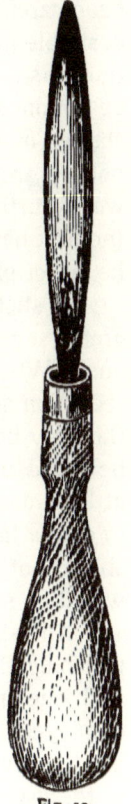

Fig. 51.

Fig. 52.

being very tough, the formation of perfectly smooth lines involves considerable skill and care. If no black line is desired the border is scratched in the etched plate. This is a much easier method. The use of a prism or reversing mirror, referred to in the next chapter, is highly desirable for half-tone negatives. For fine work, making a print on copper by asphalt and etching with perchloride of iron, as before referred to, will be found most satisfactory.

CHAPTER XII.

MISCELLANEOUS HINTS.

In the preceding chapters the zinc etching process has been carefully outlined. For a number of reasons it is the most desirable method of relief engraving. Gelatine swell and gelatine washout require skill and experience which cannot easily be obtained without long apprenticeship, and, except for certain classes of work, are not nearly so good. Therefore they will not be treated at length in the following chapters. A few words further, however, as to economical methods in working the first named process, and negatives for all of them, will not be out of place.

It should be remembered that it costs no more to photograph several drawings on the same plate than a single small one. Wherever possible, all copy having the same amount of reduction should be saved until enough has accumulated to fill the copy board. Even where this cannot be done, films should be saved until enough have accumulated to print one-third or at least one-fourth of a sheet of zinc, as it takes little more time to etch a large sheet than a small one. Rough and fine work should not, however, be put on the same piece, as the latter would be sure to suffer in the etching.

An establishment in which one man does all the work, from polishing the zinc to blocking the cut, cannot hope to compete with one in which the work is divided amongst a number of employes. Few can both photograph and etch perfectly. In most shops the work is divided into these two departments, and in the majority there are three more, viz: zinc polishing, zinc printing and blocking. Where there is sufficient to still further divide it, the best results can be obtained at the least expense. Often in small establishments it will pay better to have part of the work, such as zinc polishing, routing and blocking, done by other parties. The materials used, though sometimes expensive, are, with the exception of zinc, used in such small quantities that they do not materially affect the cost. It will not pay to economize by purchasing them of inferior quality. When such articles as etching ink, stripping solution, etc., can be obtained prepared at reasonable prices and of superior quality, it will not pay to make them. Should it be necessary to change them slightly for some special experiment, their composition can quickly be learned.

If lead pencil marks are run on the ground glass of the camera horizontally and vertically, so as to cross each other at the center, and are then marked off into inches, it will greatly facilitate the proper reduction. It is also a good idea to mark the camera slide and stand at the point where the camera will make the reduction of one-half, one-third, one-fourth and other common sizes.

But a very small proportion of the silver is actually used, as the balance runs away in the sink. Many photographers precipitate the washings in a tank, allow them to settle over night, and then drain off the water above them. The muddy precipitate is taken out at intervals and, together with the other wastes, sent to the refiner. Very few photo-engravers take the trouble to do this, but usually the blotting paper on which plates are drained, and with which the back is cleaned, and the paper or cotton through which the bath is filtered, are kept until an appreciable amount has accumulated. Should the silver bath be in very bad shape, it will often pay better to pre-cipitate by adding saturated solution of common salt until the settled water is no longer turned milky on the addition of more salt, and send it to one of the many firms who make a business of refining such wastes.

It sometimes happens that an order is received for making a plate in which the design appears white on a black ground. If the copy is on white paper, and the design opaque, it can often be used instead of a negative by placing it in contact with the sensitized metal plate in the printing frame, and giving it a somewhat longer exposure than required for an ordinary print. The paper may be rendered more transparent by soaking in turpentine and oil. If you have the original printing block, a proof may be taken on thin white paper with black ink, and rendered still more opaque by bronzing it before the ink is dry. Should a reduction be required, make a negative. From this a positive can be made by contact with another sensitized plate, but as the silver solution would spoil the negative, gelatine dry plates are best. The operator can procure plates and expose and develop them himself, but as such jobs are rare it will not pay to fit up a dark room for dry plate work, and it will generally be found more economical to have some portrait or landscape photographer make the positive. There are methods by which the print on zinc can be changed so that the white portions will appear black and the black portions white, but, as above stated, on account of the infrequency of such work it will not pay to fit up for it. If it is desired to make a cut left-handed, it can be done by printing on the zinc directly from the negative without stripping and turning it. This is sometimes very useful when making borders from original drawings, as but one-half of the design need be drawn, and two negatives having been made and stripped, one of them can be turned and both films matched closely together for making the print.

In some establishments mirrors or prisms are used to obtain reversed drawings without stripping. The idea is illustrated in Fig. 53. The camera is so mounted on an L shaped

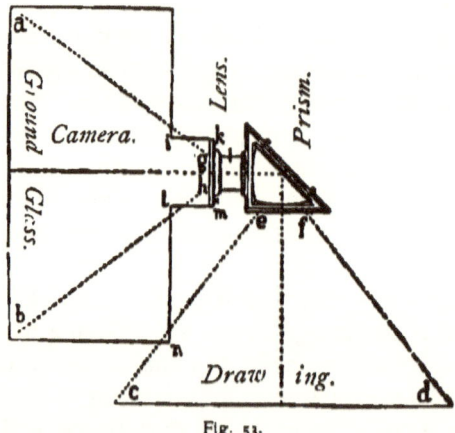

Fig. 53.

swing or stand that the opening in the prism will face the center of the copy-board. As considerable light is lost in transmission, the exposure requires from one-fifth to one-half more time than without the prism, depending upon the make and arrangement. The proper size is given the negative by moving the copy-board, not the camera, the front of which is stationary. Focusing is accomplished in the usual manner, *i. e.*, by moving the back of the camera. After drying, the negative is usually varnished to prevent its being scratched. The print is made in the frame in the usual manner. For half-tone, such negatives are preferable, as there is less danger of injury or distortion than if the film were stripped, but it is seldom used for line work on account of the longer exposure, and because it is more economical to strip the films and print a number on a large sheet of zinc than to print separately from each negative.

Zinc rapidly oxidizes in the atmosphere, and becomes covered with a gray coating. To a certain extent this will prevent further oxidation, but if kept in a damp place the plates will become coated with a white deposit, and rapidly deteriorate. If they are to be preserved for any length of time, the surface should be rubbed with a very little tallow. Another way which also adds greatly to the attractiveness is, to coat them with copper. This can be done in the battery by using a solution of cyanide of copper. It can also be accomplished by the following method. Prepare a bath by dissolving ten ounces of chloride of copper in six ounces of water. Add to this fifteen ounces concentrated water ammonia and three hundred ounces of water. This solution will have a bright blue color. Add to it concentrated solution of cyanide of potassium until the color has almost disappeared. Pour a little of this bath into a shallow tray, and in it lay the zinc etching, which has previously been carefully cleaned with benzine, and afterwards with chalk and ammonia. In a few moments it will become covered with a bright deposit of copper. Leave it in for five or ten minutes, then wash thoroughly under the tap and dry with hot sawdust. It is of course understood that the coating of copper is very thin, and therefore will not add materially to the strength of the plate, but a thick coating cannot be given without detracting from the sharpness of the cut. This preparation deteriorates rapidly and should be fresh.

Zinc is not only harder than type metal, but has more elasticity. This makes etchings much more difficult to print than electrotypes or stereotypes, and the defect is aggravated by the use of such thin metal. Whenever long runs are to be made, it will always pay to have an electrotype made from the original.

For economy's sake, nitric acid and distilled water should be purchased in carboys. An acid pump for filling bottles from them would be an excellent investment.

Stains on the fingers are almost unavoidable. Those made by acid cannot be removed except by rubbing off the epidermis with a piece of pumice stone. Silver stains caused by photography are generally removed by wetting and rubbing them with a lump of cyanide of potassium. This is a most dangerous proceeding, as the cyanide is an intense poison, and may cause sores which are difficult to heal. Although many people are not affected by it, a better way is, to mix three ounces tincture of iodine and one ounce concentrated water ammonia. When the liquid becomes clear, it is ready for use. With some people, the bichromatized zinc printing solution will also produce painful sores, and care should be exercised to prevent cutting the fingers on the glass when using it.

DRAWING ON ZINC.

It sometimes happens that there is not sufficient time to make a negative and print on zinc in the usual manner. In such cases the drawing can be made directly upon it. Procure a stick of tuche, sometimes called lithograp["]her's drawing ink (Vanhymbeck's is excellent), and rub it in a shallow dish until the bottom is covered with a thin layer. Now add a few drops of clean water and rub thoroughly together with the tip of your finger. It should be of the consistency of cream and perfectly opaque. Grain the zinc as if for etching, and draw upon it with a common steel pen. Be very careful not to touch the surface of the zinc with your fingers or anything greasy. It is best to use the retouching board for this purpose. When the ink is perfectly dry, gum up the plate as described in Chapter VIII, fan the gum dry and then roll up with No. 2 etching ink. At first the lines will disappear, leaving a bright metal surface. Gradually they will take ink and become black. In the meantime the gum sponge must be freely used, to prevent the ink from taking hold of the blank spaces. When the lines have a good coating of ink, the powder is dusted and melted on, and the etching can proceed as if the print were produced photographically. Tuche is difficult to work, and this method cannot be used on fine jobs.

SILVER PRINTS.

Preparing silver prints does not properly come within the scope of this manual, but almost every photo-engraver who does original work is required to make them. Procure a good quality of salted paper from a supply house. Prepare the silver bath by dissolving nitrate of silver in distilled water until the hydrometer registers forty-five grains to the ounce. Place this solution in a glass tray on one end of which is affixed a glass rod, and draw a paper through it in such manner that the surface of the paper will pass through the bath several times. Always select the side which is most suitable for drawing. Hang it in the dark room by means of clips. As soon as dry, it is ready for use, but some first expose it to the fumes of ammonia, as this makes it more sensitive. It should be freshly prepared every day. Make the negative once and a half or twice the size the cut is intended to be when finished. Expose the sensitized paper beneath the negative in an ordinary printing frame. The time will depend upon the light. When sufficiently exposed, wash it in a tray containing two ounces of salt dissolved in one quart of water. When the print has turned red, take it out and wash in a tray containing a solution of one ounce of hyposulphate of soda and six ounces of water. Then wash in running water for at least ten minutes. When dry, attach the print to a piece of card-board by means of starch paste. After the artist has drawn upon it, and his ink has thoroughly dried, place it in a tray containing concentrated solution bichloride of mercury in alcohol, to which add a few drops of hydrochloric acid. Rock the tray gently until the paper is bleached its original color, then remove the drawing and wash it in running water for at least five minutes. When dry, it may be returned to the artist for retouching.

THE MEZZOTYPE PROCESS.

This is the name given to a class of engravings in which the tones are produced by means of fine dots, the effect resembling, more than anything else, lithographic crayon work. There are several ways in which the work can be done. 1. The design may be drawn on stipple paper with lithographic crayon, and from this a negative made and printed on zinc in the usual manner. 2. The zinc may be grained with emery in the same manner in which a lithographic stone is roughened, and the

drawing made directly upon the zinc with crayon.   3. A half-
tone negative may be made by the intervention of a screen in
which the lines are not straight, but irregularly disposed.
4. From an ordinary negative a print may be made on a thin
sheet of gelatine, and this gelatine broken up into a grain by
mechanical or chemical means.   There is little demand for the
result of any of these processes, so they will not be described.
For certain classes of work, however, such as railroad hangers,
it is desirable to produce effects similar to those of lithography,
yet print the engravings on a type press.   In such cases the
second method above mentioned is sometimes used, but usually
the so-called mezzotype or color process is employed.   The
results will depend not only upon the operator's ability as an
etcher, but upon his skill as an artist and his knowledge of
color effects.   The width of the powdering box is somewhat
greater than that of the widest zinc plate.   The length corres-
ponds with that of the plate, and the height is the same as
the length.   To the centers of its two sides are affixed journals
which are supported by a stand.   In the front of the box, near
the bottom, is placed a small door which can be closed tightly,
and even with the bottom of the door are several rows of wire.
To operate the box, a small amount of powder is put in it.
Ordinary dragon's blood will answer, but many prefer one
which is made up of mastic, asphaltum and bees-wax, melted
together and powdered.   The box is revolved a number of
times, so that the powder will be agitated and thoroughly distributed throughout the interior.   The box is then fastened into
position and allowed to rest for a few minutes until the coarser
particles of the powder have settled at the bottom.   The door
is opened and the zinc plate slid in upon the wire face upwards.
After a few moments the plate is removed, when its surface
will be found covered with small bits of powder evenly distributed.   If the tint is not dark enough, the plate is replaced
and allowed to remain until enough powder has fallen.   It is
then carefully taken to the etchers' oven and heated thoroughly.
Great care must be exercised at this point.   If the heating is
carried too far, the spaces between the dots will be covered
with a resinous distillation from the powder, and will resist the
acid.   If not heated sufficiently, the powder will not adhere well
enough to protect the metal.   After heating, the plate should

have a velvety appearance, the dots partly hanging together and showing the bare zinc between them. The etching is done in the usual manner with weak acid and without brushing. If very coarse dots are desired, coarse powder must be used, but it should also be noted that the longer the box is allowed to rest before introduction of the plate, the finer will be the dots, as the coarser particles will settle at the bottom first. The above procedure is employed when a plate of even tint is desired. Its use is limited, being sometimes applied to making borders around zinc etchings, in which case the border is first painted over with lithographic ink dissolved in turpentine, and after the cut is completed the ink is washed off and the design itself painted over, so as to leave the balance of the zinc ready to receive the mezzotint powder. It is also used in cases where the proof of a finished half-tone engraving shows a back-ground or sky which is too dark. After protecting the body of the engraving from the acid in the usual manner, the plate is powdered and again etched. For color work the design of the black or key plate is generally transferred to the surface of the zinc by making a print from the negative and powdering in the usual manner. A slight etch is made, after which the surface is cleaned, leaving the design in bright lines on a dull surface. If there is no negative of the key plate, take a proof on stout paper and place its face in contact with a zinc plate. Now run the plate and proof through a lithographic hand press under strong pressure. Enough ink will be transferred to the surface of the metal to permit its being powdered and etched as before. After cleaning, the artist paints the plate with etching ink and turpentine, excepting only such parts as he desires shall not print at all but remain white. After powdering and melting, these spaces are etched and routed out in the usual manner. The plate is again cleaned, and this time the artist paints in the parts which he intends shall be solid or black. After dusting these parts with powder the plate is placed in the dusting box and sufficient powder allowed to settle upon it to give a moderately dark tone. The etching is performed in the usual manner. It will be noted that the resulting plate will have but three tones. Solid black, white, and a gray middle tone. If it is desired to make variations in this last tone, such parts of it as are right may, after the first etch, be painted over with etching ink and turpentine, and powdered, after which the plate is placed in the acid, which will lighten the dots of the remaining surface by slightly under-cutting the edges. By painting and powdering over additional portions, still lighter tones may be secured in parts by a third etch. This procedure must be repeated for each color block. The beautiful color work of French illustrated papers is the result of a combination of the above method with half-tone. The copy is usually a wash drawing or a painting. From this are made a number of half-tone negatives. For the black or key plate a cross line screen is invariably used, but for the lighter color plates a single diagonal lined screen is often chosen. After making the prints on zinc the artist strengthens such parts as he desires shall produce solid tones and scrapes out the high lights. . If very light tints are desired the plate is dusted in after the half-tone plate has been etched, and in this way a tint plate produced which will not interfere with the lines of the key. Such parts as are desired solid must of course be painted over. Considerable skill and judgment are necessary to obtain good effects, and unless the operator is thoroughly acquainted with color work the results are almost certain to be unsatisfactory.

CHAPTER XIII.

DOUBLE WASHOUT GELATINE ENGRAVING.

As compared with zinc etching, all gelatine methods are slower and more difficult. The washout processes are perhaps the most desirable. Nevertheless it takes at least eight hours to produce a cut, and the process cannot be economically worked, except in establishments where a large quantity of work is done, so that some is constantly under way, and in every stage of completion. A single cut would cost far more than a single zinc etching. Besides this, gelatine is difficult to handle, atmospheric conditions and temperature affecting the work to a great extent, so that only in a well fitted room can a man of long experience do good work economically. The gelatine plate can be used for printing small editions, but is comparatively fragile, therefore an electrotype should be taken from the original. This involves the ownership, or at least the proximity, of such a plant. While all classes and grades of work can be done, it is particularly adapted to the reproduction of book plates. Even on ordinary type matter, the cost of producing a plate is less than that of composition, and where foreign quotations or accents are frequent, or where there are engravings in the text, the gain is large. The cheap American editions of the Encyclopedia Britannica, and the reprint of Webster's Unabridged Dictionary, may be cited as works which were economically reproduced by this process.

In the simplest form of the process, the sheet of gelatine, after exposure to sunlight, is brushed out but once to procure the necessary relief. This will be treated of in the next chapter. In the double washout method, after a small amount of relief has been obtained the blank spaces or whites are filled with some opaque substance, and the sheet again exposed to the light, so that the rays will penetrate deeper and allow a second washing, which gives greater relief without danger of losing the lines. It is but fair to add that the idea of using an opaque paste was originated by Wm. Mumler, of Boston, Mass., who, on May 18th, 1875, obtained a patent. A number of photo-engraving establishments have adopted the idea, and as the patent expires upon the 18th of May, 1892, it may be used by anyone after that date without fear of trouble.

The photograph gallery should be fitted up in exactly the same manner as for zinc-etching, and the negative should be made as described in former chapters. The work room should be commodious and in as cool and dry a place as possible. All light should be excluded except such as passes through what is commonly known as yellow post-office paper. A better but more expensive way is, to glaze the windows with orange glass, and also cover them with yellow muslin curtains mounted on spring rollers. Beneath the work table there should be a series of drawers large enough to hold sheets of gelatine of sizes equal to the largest piece of work which it is intended to do. There should also be a large, deep sink provided with running water, and having cross-bars a few inches from the top, on which the gelatine sheets may be rested while washing out. Alongside the sink should be a large table for the dishes and trays, and above it, shelves for chemicals. A small closet should be partitioned off. In this the gelatine is to be rotted. The following utensils or apparatus must also be made or purchased.

THE DRYING BOX.

The size and construction of this will depend entirely upon the location and the scale on which the work is to be carried on. Large establishments devote the entire side of the room to a series of shelves, through which dry air is drawn by means of an exhaust fan. For experimental purposes, a large wooden box having level shelves three inches apart, each of them four or five inches wider one way than the setting frames described further on, and having open spaces at alternate ends of the shelves, so that the air will pass over the surface of every plate, will do very nicely. The front of the box should be provided with a door which can be closed air tight. In the top and bottom of the box are openings, and beneath the lower one is placed a gas or oil heater. Fig. 54 shows a construction adapted to large establishments having power. The end which opens into the work room is provided with a muslin covered opening, M.

At the other end, in the closet A, is set a rotary fan which draws the air through the screen so that it passes over the

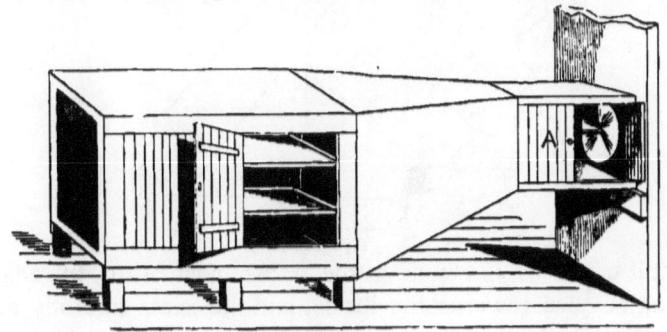

Fig. 54.

plates and out of the window at the end of the closet.

SETTING FRAMES.

These are made of the finest plate glass one-quarter inch thick, perfectly level, and free from flaws. For large work they may be 26x26 inches, so that one will answer for a pound of gelatine. For experimental work, 10x12 will do. Around each glass is a frame of ash or other hard wood, attached in the same manner as the wooden rim of a school-boy's slate, the edges being slightly beveled towards the inside, as illustrated in Fig. 55. The wood should project five-eighths of an inch

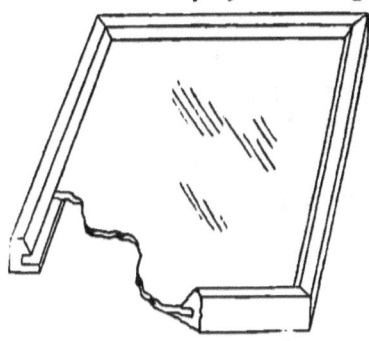

Fig. 55.

above the surface of the glass. Should the joints be imperfect, they must be filled with wax, otherwise the gelatine will creep into the cracks and dry, and may at some future time absorb moisture and swell so as to crack the glass or twist the frame out of shape. Before using, the woodwork should be well waxed, otherwise the gelatine will run up the sides and harden, adhering so firmly to the wood as to necessitate cutting into it.

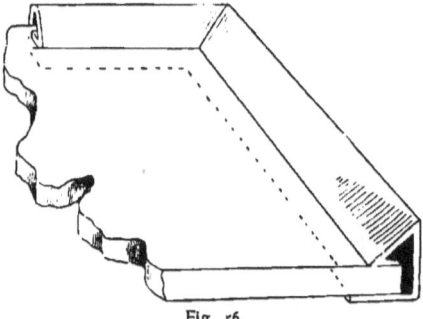

Fig. 56.

A still better way is to have the frame made of tin, the edges being beveled towards the inside, and the joints carefully and smoothly made.   This construction is shown in Fig. 56.

LEVELING TABLE.

This is a frame-work about three feet high provided with a number of stringers through which thumb-screws pass—twice as many in the back as in the front.   The frames just described are laid on three screws, the frame-work extending beyond them.

ROTTING DISHES.

These are earthenware bowls such as used for mixing dough and batter.   Generally yellow-ware is used, as it is least expensive.   They should hold one or two gallons each, and quite a number should be kept on hand.

POURING DISH.

This is similar to those described above, except that it has a lip provided with a fine wire gauze strainer attached by means of a band of tin around the upper edge.

FILTER CLOTH.

This is made of heavy, brown drilling, one yard square. It should be hemmed on the edges to prevent fraying.   Boil it thoroughly and wring out before using.

WASHOUT BRUSHES.

These are similar in shape to watch-makers' cleaning brushes, the brush portion being about four inches long, and of medium stiff bristles.   The best will be found most economical, as in the cheaper grades the bristles will soften and lie down when wet. For the first washing a brush with three or four rows will answer, but for brushing away the black paste and giving the second washout, brushes having eight or ten lines of bristles are more economical.

ALCOHOL TRAYS.

These should be deep trays, and are preferably of porcelain or glass. Rubber trays will answer very nicely, and the coated wooden trays known as "common sense" can also be made to answer. It is economical to have them large, so that they will hold a large quantity of alcohol, otherwise they will absorb water from the gelatine and soon require replacing. If rubber or wooden trays are employed, the alcohol must be poured back into the bottle immediately after using, and the tray thoroughly washed with warm water until the greasy appearance has left it, otherwise the alcohol will soften the rubber and cause it to warp or blister.

SQUEEGEE ROLLER.

A rubber roller provided with a handle, and from six to twelve inches long, should be purchased. Its use will be described further on. A clothes wringer can be utilized for the same purpose.

SPATULAS.

There should be at least three of these of different sizes. They are used in removing the gelatine from the zinc after electrotypes have been made, mixing and applying the filling-in paste, cleaning dishes, and for numerous other purposes.

PRINTING FRAMES,

For small or experimental work the ordinary photographers' deep printing frame, provided with wedges to place beneath

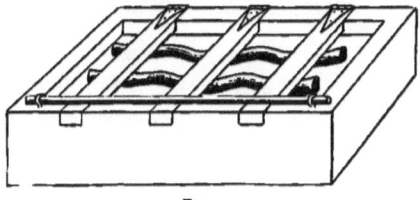

Fig. 57.

the springs, will answer nicely. For large work a heavy frame similar to that used for printing on zinc, or of the construction shown in Fig. 57, is preferable. It must be deep enough to admit the pressure bag. During cold weather a piece of heavy felt or chinchilla cloth is placed between the pressure board and the gelatine when printing. In warm weather the heat of the sun is apt to melt the gelatine, causing it to creep or to stick to the negative. To obviate this a rubber pressure bag must be provided. It should be perfectly square at all corners, flat on the surfaces, and should fit neatly into the printing frame. Immediately before using, it is filled with cold water and substituted for the felt, thus reducing the temperature of the gelatine while the print is being made.

PRINTING BOXES.

These are boxes made of light wood, open at both ends, one of which fits closely on the printing frame. The usual length is three or four feet. They are painted black on the inside. When exposing the gelatine, the tube is fitted over the frame, the opening of which is pointed to the light. Its use will prevent side rays from penetrating the gelatine and rendering it insoluble between the lines. The best construction is one in which the box is mounted on trunnions so as to make adjustment easy.

PRINTING BOARD.

This is an ordinary board provided with a small projection at one end, and painted black. On this the prints are placed after being filled in with paste for the second printing. Its use obviates changing each print so as to face the light as the sun changes position, and is also more convenient for handling the prints, as the board can be lifted and a number carried about without danger of their sticking together.

TALC BOX.

This is an ordinary tin spice box. It is filled with finest talc.

PUMICE STONE BOX.

This is similar to the above. It is filled with the finest powdered pumice and should be labeled so as to be distinguished from the talc box.

ROTTING BOX.

A good size for this box is two and a half feet square and six feet high. It is lined on the interior with zinc, sheet iron or tin, so separated from the walls as to allow a draft of cool air to circulate in the empty space, thereby preventing danger of fire. Fig. 58 shows the usual construction. At the top are three shelves upon which are set the earthenware dishes containing the gelatine which is being rotted. In the door are set panes of glass A A, which permit inspection of the

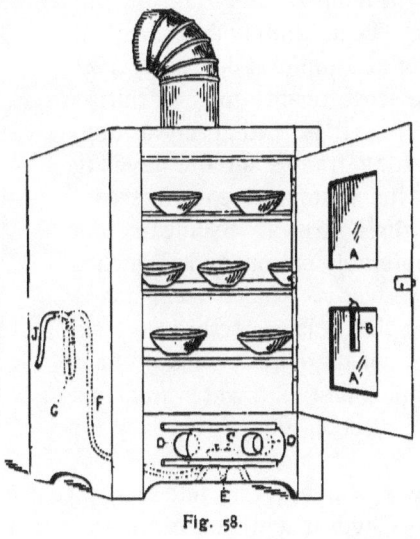

Fig. 58.

interior, also a thermometer B, which can be seen from the outside. C is a sliding board at the bottom, so arranged as to permit the closing of the holes D D, thus regulating the draft. E represents the gas heating stove, which is connected by the hose F to the regulator G, and from thence to the supply pipe. Fig. 59 shows an enlarged view of the regulator which is attached to the inside of the box by a band of brass. It is made of a heavy tube of hard glass. Into the neck is fitted a rubber stopper 3, through which two smaller bent tubes 1 and 2 are passed. At the bottom of the test tube is placed some mercury. It will be noticed that the bottom of the exit tube is ground off at an acute angle. To set the regulator, the gas is lit and the tube 2 pushed up or down until the thermometer remains at 120°. The tube can then be marked at the proper point with a sharp file. There are a number of other articles which will be mentioned further on.

When everything is in order, procure a pound of Nelson's amber gelatine in shreds, place it in one of the rotting dishes and pour on enough filtered or distilled water to cover it well.

About three and one-half pints will be right. Allow it to stand until it has absorbed the water and swelled. Turn the mass occasionally, otherwise it may dry in places. When thoroughly soaked, place the dish in the rotting box and carefully note the temperature. The amount of rotting cannot be accurately described. If the heat is kept at a uniform degree of 120° F. it will take from twenty-four to thirty-six hours. While it is rotting, lay a number of the setting frames on the leveling table so that the bottom of each piece of glass rests on three screws. By means of a spirit level, preferably of iron, and six inches long, level it perfectly. When the glass is in position, see that it is perfectly free from dirt or grease. If there is any doubt about this matter, wipe it first with water ammonia and then with alcohol, when it is ready for waxing. Procure some pure, unrefined,

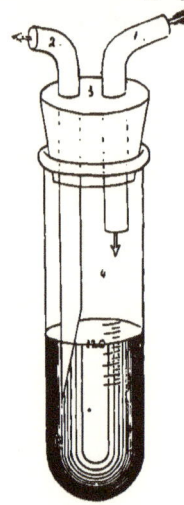

Fig. 59.

yellow bees-wax, shave it very fine and place it in a glass-stoppered bottle. Cover it with concentrated sulphuric ether and shake until it is dissolved. Continue adding wax until no more will be dissolved. This is the stock bottle. For use, dilute it with equal parts of ether and alcohol. Shake well, and it is ready for use. The exact strength of this solution is not of moment. A solution of wax in benzole may be substituted. To wax the plate, pour some of the mixture upon the glass, holding the bottle in the left hand, and with a bit of cotton flannel, twill side out, held in the right hand, rub with a circular motion as though putting a French polish on hard wood. Never let the cloth stop, and when raising it do so with a straight swing. Should the wax chill and accumulate in spots, dampen a cloth with a little of the ether and alcohol mixture, and rub until the milky appearance has entirely left it, leaving a fine lustre.

Powder four drams potassium bichromate in a mortar, and add two ounces warm water and from one-half to one dram of water ammonia. Some operators use bichromate of ammonium, omitting the water ammonia; others use a mixture of both. This is the sensitizing solution. When the gelatine is sufficiently rotted (something difficult to describe, but readily dis-

cernible to the experienced operator by its odor), add the above
quantity to the gelatine in the bowl, stirring constantly. Now
add about two ounces of glycerine, which gives flexibility to
the sheet. The quantity depends considerably on the temperature and the humidity of the atmosphere. Should too much be
added, it will, particularly in hot weather, lessen the sensitiveness and the solubility of the parts unacted upon by the light.
It will also cause the objectionable "creeping" which will be
described further on. If, however, the quantity is insufficient,
the sheet will be so brittle as to crack and split while being cut
with the shears, although in this case the difficulty can often
be overcome by warming the sheet before cutting. Assure
yourself that the setting frames are thoroughly coated, perfectly
level and clean. Gather the straining cloth by the four corners and, holding it over the pouring dish, pour the warm gelatine into it. It will come through with difficulty, and must be
forced by twisting the bag in the same manner as adopted in
domestic establishments when straining starch or jelly. Take
a small piece of clean card-board about the size of a visiting
card, rounded at the corners, dampen slightly with warm water,
and with it skim the bubbles to one side of the dish and rake
them over the side of the bowl into the water. See that the
gelatine is perfectly clean. Pour into the setting frames either
by beginning at the center and pouring with a circular motion
until the frame is full, or pouring on one side and tilting the
frame so as to allow the gelatine to flow evenly and smoothly
until it reaches the other side. If the gelatine be too cold or
too thick it will set unevenly and in ridges, and if these faults
be pronounced, it will not flow to the edges before it sets. If
it is too warm, it is liable to melt the wax and make the sheet
of gelatine adhere to the glass when dry, ruining it. The top
of the sheet should be as level and smooth as the bottom.
Should air bubbles appear, remove them by touching with the
dampened finger. A little experience will determine the proper
consistency and temperature. The quantity in the formula
will cover about six hundred and seventy-five square inches.
Allow the frames to stand until the gelatine has set. This can be
determined by dampening the finger and touching the surface.
It should be pliable but not sticky. Now place the frames in
the drying closet. It is best that the moistened air be carried

outside of the building. If it is well constructed the sheets should be sufficiently dried in forty-eight hours. If the drying is carried on longer than four or five days, the quality will deteriorate and but little relief can be secured from the plates. It is advisable to turn the plates end for end twice a day, so that all parts will be equally exposed to the current of fresh air. When the gelatine is dry, remove it from the glass. If the above operations have been carefully performed, it should part easily after a knife or spatula has been run around the edges of the frame. Should it be removed forcibly, it is liable to take part of the glass with it, ruining the frame. In such cases the cause is generally, solution which is too hot, improper waxing of the glass, or too much moisture in the air passing through the drying box. When the sheets are dried, trim off the rough edges with a pair of wall-paperer's shears and pile them up, placing a sheet of blotting paper between every two sheets of gelatine, then place in the drawer of the work table and put a flat board on the pile, sufficiently weighted to keep the sheets from warping. The sheets should be about one-sixteenth of an inch thick, perfectly smooth and even. When ready to print, cut off a piece of gelatine a trifle larger than your negative. Rub with talc the surface which was upon the glass of the setting frame, dusting off the surplus powder with a camel hair brush. Upon the glass of the printing frame lay the negative with the film uppermost. Upon the negative place the gelatine talced side down. Then lay the pad of felt above it. In warm weather use the pressure pad, and finally force down the back sufficiently to bring the gelatine in contact with the negative. For coarse work, the frame may be exposed directly to sunlight. Where the lines are close together, the printing box should be fitted over its edges, and the opening pointed towards the light. This will make the light strike perpendicularly and prevent the lines from becoming heavier or running into each other. Where the color is evenly distributed, as in type matter, the entire surface will require about the same relief, and a plain exposure is sufficient. Where, however, it varies greatly, as in some wood engravings, a short exposure would not give sufficient relief to the isolated lines, while a long one would make the darker portions too heavy, as even with the printing box some light would diffuse, causing the lines to run into each other. In work of this character it is best to cover the glass of the printing frame immediately above the darker portions of the copy, which in the negative are most transparent. This can best be accomplished by applying with a brush some opaque pigment, such as venetian red, to which is added a very small amount of gum arabic dissolved in water. After an exposure, which is judged to be about two-thirds of that required for the lighter portions of the cut, the opaque pigment is carefully cleaned off and another exposure made. For subjects which require fine execution, and in which there is great variance of color, this plan can be further elaborated. Three, four, or even a dozen different exposures, securing for each part the proper amount of light.

It is impossible to name the length of time required for an exposure. It will vary with the light, and with the composition and age of the gelatine sheets. Generally five minutes is sufficient, but it will vary from two to twenty minutes. When the print is finished, carry the frame into the operating room and allow it to cool before removing the gelatine, otherwise there is danger of spoiling the negative. Remove the back of the frame, place the left hand upon the gelatine and, taking hold of one corner with the right, gently raise it from the negative, in the meantime sliding the left hand towards the opposite corner to prevent its slipping. A little care will prevent the loss of the negative. In practice, a number of prints are allowed to accumulate, being placed in another drawer and weighted down as before directed, to prevent their curling. When warm, they are particularly liable to warp out of shape.

The washing out must be rapidly performed, and as the manipulation is a delicate one, experience alone will render the operator proficient. Fill a rubber tray with cold water and in it lay a sheet of plate glass a trifle larger than the print. With the left hand tip the gelatine under the surface with the unexposed side next the glass and, raising both sheets together, press the water from between them. This operation must be performed very rapidly, for should water be left between the sheets, it would cause the gelatine to swell, and develop in the subsequent manipulations a number of serious faults, such as loss of fine details and curling of lines. Gelatine which has been treated as directed is not nearly so liable to swell as otherwise, nevertheless this tendency cannot be entirely over-come. Lay the glass to which the gelatine is affixed on a block of wood resting on the slides in the center of the sink, and pass over the surface with some alcohol. This removes all moisture or grease, and is particularly necessary when oil has been used instead of talc to prevent the negative from adhering. In the meantime, the water for washing out should have been heated about as hot as the hand can stand with comfort. Alongside of it should be another basin of cold water. Grasp the wash-out brush in your right hand, dip it in the hot water and pass it firmly and freely with a circular motion over the entire sur-face, frequently renewing the water until the required depth is obtained without undermining the finer lines. If the work is at all fine, the greater portion should have sufficient relief for printing. When this is obtained, remove the gelatine from the glass and quickly dip into the cold water. Remove it as rapidly as possible, shake and drain the superfluous moisture from it, and immerse it immediately in the tray which rests alongside of the sink, and which is filled with wood alcohol. In a few minutes it may be removed from this tray and placed in the second one containing fresher alcohol which has not absorbed water from frequent dippings. In this it should remain ten or fifteen minutes. Now take the gelatine from the tray and allow the surface to dry. If the work is in a hurry, evaporation may be hastened by fanning. The gelatine is now ready for re-mounting for the second washout. Select a piece of thin plate glass a little larger than the cut and lay it upon the table. Paint the back of the gelatine with shellac. It is best to pre-pare this yourself by soaking fresh unbleached shellac in pure alcohol for several days until dissolved. Apply with a fine camel hair brush in a thin even coating. When it becomes tacky, place it against the glass. Lay a piece of blotting paper over it and pass the squeegee roller from the center of the cut to the outer edges, pressing out the superfluous shellac. Remove the blotter, wipe the edges clean, and proceed with the next cut. Place one above the other with a weight on top, and allow the pile to dry as long as possible. In the meantime prepare the blacking-in paste. For this, soak an ounce of fish glue or white gelatine in eight or ten ounces of water, and when thoroughly swelled, dissolve in a water bath. Add from one to two drams of glycerine and a few drops of carbolic acid to prevent its rotting. This is the stock bottle. In another bottle have some Porto Rico molasses. It should be of good body, not too thin. In a convenient receptacle have some of the finest ground lamp black. When everything is in readiness, warm the gelatine in a water bath. Fill a shallow tin pan with hot water and lay a piece of heavy sheet zinc above the bath. The heat of the water will keep the zinc warm and prevent the paste from setting. Pour some of the melted gelatine upon the zinc, and alongside of it, a little of the molasses. The exact proportions cannot be given—about two of the former and one of the latter. With a small, steel spatula, grind and mix them thoroughly together. Now take some lamp black and work it into the mixture until the paste is soft, velvety and perfectly opaque. As the ingredients vary greatly, nothing but experience can determine their proportions. If too much gelatine is used, it is liable to set too quickly, necessitating too much friction when wiping it off. If there is too much molasses, it is liable to remain soft and wipe out from between the lines. If too little lamp black has been used, the mass will not be opaque, but will allow the light to penetrate it. If too much has been added, the paste will lack cohesion and crack in drying, so that the light will enter the fissures. When the mass is of the proper consistency, apply it with the spatula to the surface of the washed out cut, filling the spaces between the lines and remov- ing the surplus with the same tool, taking care not to injure the lines with its edge. The character of the work should be plainly discernible through the thin coating which in places adheres to the surface. Allow the paste to set, but not harden. Take a damp cloth—portions of old linen or cotton clothing without nap and worn soft are preferable—and, holding it in the right hand, rub with the ball of the second finger only, keep- ing the rest of the cloth from the surface with the first and third fingers. Never wipe over the surface twice with the same spot of cloth, and, while avoiding the removal of paste between the lines, see that the surface is perfectly clean. It is best to give a final cleaning with a piece of cloth which has not before been used for the purpose. This can be used for the first rubbing of the next plate. Immediately after use, throw the rags in a basin of warm water, which will soften the paste so that they can be wrung out and used again. Should the large spaces be unavoidably emptied, they can be filled in with a small brush dipped into the warm paste. Hold the sheet up to the light, and when an examination shows that the surface is perfectly clean, and all the spaces between the lines are filled, lay the sheet upon the printing board, and place this in such position that the light strikes it at right angles to its surface. The second exposure will be somewhat longer than the first, and will vary from twenty to sixty minutes. After the second printing take the plate to the sink, and with a brush used for this purpose only, wash out the black paste. Then with the heavy washout brush proceed to give the cut the required relief, taking care not to continue the operation long enough to undermine the lines or cause them to curl very much. This operation will loosen the shellac, so that after plunging it in the cold water the gelatine can easily be removed by passing the spatula beneath it. It should then be quickly placed in the alcohol as before. Do not allow it to remain long in the first tray, otherwise it will swell by absorbing water with which the alcohol has been diluted from previous plates. There is no limit to the time at which it may be placed in the second tray, which contains fresh and pure alcohol. The contents of the second tray may be used for the first washing the following day. When the sheet has hardend, remove it from the tray, allow the alcohol to drain back into it, and wipe the back so as to remove the shellac which still adheres. The cut is now ready for mounting. For this purpose, zinc blanks are best adapted. They should be perfectly flat and smooth, slightly larger than the gelatine sheet, but need not be of high grade metal. Rub the surface with the No. 1 sand paper until it is bright and clean, coat the gelatine with a thin, even coat of shellac, and fasten it to the surface of the zinc in the same way as it was before attached to the glass. Be careful to avoid air bubbles between the plates, as these may cause defective electrotypes. Place a number of sheets above each other and weight down until dry. This operation is usually performed at the close of the day's work, so that the blocks may harden over night. If all the manipulations have been carefully performed, the plates will have plenty of relief and be hard and firm throughout. A proof should now be taken and, if found correct, the plate sent to the electrotyper, who proceeds to reproduce it in metal in the usual manner. When a printing plate has been obtained, the gelatine can be removed from the zinc, and the latter again used after being polished. It is sometimes desirable to keep the gelatine plates, in which case some care must be exercised, as the gelatine is very brittle. The removal can be accomplished without breakage by applying a clean, flat spatula to one edge and then another, and finally sliding it quickly between the two sheets. As has before been noted, the gelatine processes are comparatively difficult and, except in the hands of an expert, uncertain. The most frequent difficulties are those mentioned below.

CREEPING.

This is the technical name for the condition in which the lines run into each other as if the light had penetrated through the opaque parts of the negative. When washing out, the lines will either be removed entirely or remain in a solid black mass. This may be caused by the gelatine sheet not being sufficiently dry, or too much glycerine having been added to the mixture, but generally these faults will cause little trouble unless accentuated by the usual cause—too much heat from the sun. Very often this can be remedied by the use of the water bag. If, however, this fails to remove the trouble, throw away the gelatine and prepare a fresh batch.

CURLING OF LINES.

Noticeable while washing and always present to a slight extent. Generally due to gelatine having been insufficiently rotted, thereby requiring more time and longer brushing with hot water to obtain the desired depth. It may also be caused by the presence of too much glycerine or improperly dried sheets. The alcohol bath will remedy it to a great extent, and the addition to it of a little saturated solution of alum will greatly facilitate matters. If, however, the gelatine is properly prepared, alum should never be used.

INSOLUBILITY.

Caused by too long drying in a damp atmosphere, extreme age of the gelatine, or exposure to light. It can be tested by dampening a piece with tepid water and rubbing between the fingers. It should melt away at this temperature without in the least swelling before dissolving. If it is flexible and clear, and'shows this solubility, it should produce good cuts. It sometimes happens that the entire surface of the cut will not readily yield to the washout brush. In such cases, sprinkle a little of the fine pumice stone upon the surface and rub with the palm of the hand until the fine polish has disappeared. Some engravers prefer fine emery cloth, on which is rubbed a little tallow to prevent its scratching. Before proceeding to wash out, it should be rubbed with alcohol as heretofore directed.

GELATINE ADHERING TO NEGATIVE.

Often caused by the gelatine or negative not being thoroughly dry. Look carefully to this and rub the surface of the former with talc before placing them together. Another cause is, too much heat during exposure. The water-bag will obviate this.

CHAPTER XIV.

Single Washout Methods.

The complications involved in the operation of the method described in the previous chapter have led to many efforts towards simplification. Some have tried to overcome the tedious rotting and its attending bad odors, others have labored to perfect a method by which the necessary relief could be obtained without the assistance of blacking-in paste, second printing or hot water. Perhaps the most successful method is that known in Europe as Leimtypy. From the following short description it will be noted that in general outline it resembles the double washout method, and wherever the operations are not explicitly described it is to be understood that they are performed in the same manner. Some of the recipes, such as for cements, merely take the place of those previously described, and may, if thought desirable, be substituted for them when working the double washout process.

Soak three and one-half ounces of Nelson's amber gelatine in seven ounces of water for five or six hours. Then place it in a rice boiler and keep it at a temperature of from 140° to 150° until a flocculent precipitate takes place, leaving the gelatine clear. This may take fifteen hours. Always keep the vessel well covered, to prevent the formation of a skin on the surface of the liquid. Cool the gelatine to about 100° and add a little glycerine. The quantity will vary according to the humidity of the atmosphere, and will generally be about five drams in summer and three or four drams in winter. Too much will make the printing plate soft. Too little will cause concavity of the lines. Dissolve one ounce bichromate of potash in sixteen ounces of water and add carbonate of ammonium until all effervescence ceases. The quantity will probably be about one ounce. This solution is to be kept in a stock bottle and two drams of it are added to the above quantity of gelatine under constant stirring. In another bottle dissolve fifty grains of chromic acid in ten ounces of water. Add two ounces of this solution to the gelatine bowl. Now beat the white of an egg in one ounce of water, warm it to about 100° and add to the gelatine bowl. The emulsion is now to be strained through the filtering cloth into the straining vessel or graduate. The quantity before mentioned will be sufficient for covering a setting frame 11 x 14 inches. A temperature of 100° is best for pouring, and the vessel or graduate should be heated so as not to chill the gelatine below this point. When set, the frame should be taken to the drying closet. The sheets should be dry in fifteen or eighteen hours, but the best results will be obtained if dried forty-eight hours, when the gelatine should still be flexible enough not to break when bent. The exposure varies according to the negative, light and character of the work. It will generally take ten to thirty minutes. If an electrotype is to be made, the gelatine can be mounted on the type metal blank by means of ordinary glue, which should be tacky before the film is laid on and squeegeed to its surface. If, however, the gelatine is to be used for a printing plate, dissolve one part of rubber in fifty parts of chloroform and add three parts of mastic. Coat a piece of zinc thickly with this solution, and when dried heat it over the gas stove until the coating has melted, and while still hot lay the gelatine upon it and squeegee them tightly together. When the gelatine and mounting metal are securely fastened, take the plate to the sink. In the meantime, prepare a saturated solution of bichromate of potash, and with a soft brush pass the cold liquid over the film. In a few minutes the parts which have not been exposed to light will commence to dissolve. It should not require more than ten minutes rubbing to secure the necessary relief. When the finer lines appear to weaken, wash thoroughly under the tap, drain for a few moments and then lay in a dish of wood alcohol. The relief will turn white and the wrinkled lines will straigthen out. After laying in the alcohol for ten minutes take out the plate and allow it to dry. If the relief is insufficient, the washout operation may be repeated after an hour's time. If it is intended to print directly from the plate, the large white spaces are routed out with a chisel or routing tool, and the zinc attached to a wood block by means of tacks.

Another method which is also productive of very good results, and is quicker, is operated as follows: Place one pound of Chalmer's granulated gelatine in a rice kettle and pour upon it about three pints of water. After it has absorbed all the water, which should be in about half an hour, keep the water in the lower part of the kettle boiling for at least one hour, at the end of which time the gelatine should have a slight odor of decomposition. Take it from the fire and allow it to cool to about 100°. In a porcelain mortar grind half or three-fourths of an ounce carbonate of ammonium and add from three to four ounces of water. Add from two drams to one-half an ounce of stronger water ammonia. Then add, a small quantity at a time, from one-half to three-fourths of an ounce of chromic acid. After the effervescence has subsided, pour the solution in the bowl while constantly stirring. The gelatine must be stirred until all frothing subsides, when it should be of a yellowish milky appearance. It will be noticed that this formula is not exact. The amounts of the ingredients will vary with the stage of decomposition, light, humidity, and other points which tend to make all gelatine methods extremely difficult. Now add about two ounces of glycerine and proceed in exactly the same manner as in the double washout process, except that the sheet is permanently mounted on the metal blank before the first washout. Wash with warm water, using a stiff brush for the first few rubs, and afterwards a finer one. Lay in the alcohol tray and then allow to dry. The relief should be sufficient for printing, although the large white spaces must be routed out or built up in the mould by the electrotyper.

CHAPTER XV.

SWELLED GELATINE ENGRAVING.

Engraving by this process is slower and more expensive than zinc-etching, and, except for the reproduction of old engravings where it is difficult to obtain dense negatives, it is not recommended. Besides this, the manipulation is much more delicate, and it requires more experience to obtain good results. For these reasons it has become almost obsolete.

The negatives are made in exactly the same manner as for the preceding methods, but are not stripped, the double casting operation making the proof appear like the copy. In a porcelain lined glue pot place half an ounce of Nelson's photographic gelatine No. 1 and add seven ounces distilled water. Allow it to stand until the gelatine swells and becomes soft, then heat until it is dissolved. Test frequently with the thermometer, being careful that the temperature does not exceed 120° Fahr. When entirely dissolved, add thirty-two minims of a saturated solution of bichromate of ammonia, stir thoroughly and raise the temperature to 120°, keeping it at that heat for five minutes. It is then filtered through muslin into a graduate which has been warmed to the same degree of heat. In the meantime a number of glass plates should have been carefully cleaned. Pieces of plate glass about a quarter of an inch in thickness, perfectly flat, free from scratches, and a little larger than the negative, are best adapted to the purpose. They must be carefully leveled by means of screws beneath them, and warmed to the temperature of the solution. Enough solution is poured upon each plate to cover it well without running over the edges. They are then removed to a dark room or cupboard through which a current of air of 95° is made to circulate until the gelatine is perfectly dry. The plates are then ready for exposure, and will keep in good condition for some time. The ordinary deep printing frame used by photographers answers very well for making the print. The negative and gelatine are placed face to face in the frame, and the wedges forced in so as to bring them in contact. The exposure in good sunlight will be about fifteen minutes, or in diffused light, about one hour. When it is thought that the print is sufficiently strong, it is removed from the frame and placed in a shallow tray containing clear, cool water. The swelling begins immediately, and its progress can be ascertained by feeling with the finger tips. Considerable experience is required to ascertain the proper length of time the swelling should be allowed to continue. When it has reached a point where the design is the depth of a four-ply card-board beneath the field, the lines should still be flat upon the surface. Should the development be allowed to proceed too far, the edges of the lines will absorb water and in the finished design the surface of each line will be convex. If not swelled sufficiently, the relief will be shallow and the surface of the lines slightly concave. When it is judged that the relief is sufficient, remove from the pan, and after washing under the tap immediately place it in another pan containing a saturated solution of iron sulphate. Allow it to remain for three minutes, then remove and wash thoroughly. Now lay it on a level slab and place iron bars, half an inch in thickness, about one inch from the edges of the glass, and parallel with them. In an earthen milk pan pour a little water and add enough of the finest plaster of paris to make it the consistency of syrup. Be sure to add enough plaster, as in case the mixture is too thick water can be added without doing any harm. A little salt is usually dissolved in the water, as it makes the plaster set quickly and lessens its liability to crack when casting. Work the mixture well with the !hand. This must be thoroughly yet rapidly done, otherwise the plaster will set during the operation. Pour this mixture into the space between the bars, being careful to avoid air bubbles, which will make holes in the cast. When the plaster commences to set, scrape with a straight edge, so that the surface is level with the bearers. When set hard, run the edge of the knife beneath one end, prying the glass and plate apart. The cast is then trimmed and its edges beveled, leaving it an inch or two wider than the design. Flow the cast several times with a mixture prepared by adding one and one-half ounces silicate of soda to twenty ounces of water and then wash well under the tap.   Lay it face upwards on the casting slab and place type high bearers around the four sides.   Plaster of paris is mixed as before directed, poured into the space, and leveled even with the bars.   When hard, the two casts can easily be separated with a spatula.   The metal cast is made in an electrotypers' furnace provided with a casting pan (Fig. 60) which by means

Fig. 60.

of a crane can be swung into the furnace or into the adjoining cooling box.   The pan is heated in the metal and placed on a leveling block alongside the furnace.   In the pan is placed the float, which has also been heated.   On this are arranged the plaster casts face downwards.   There should be enough to fill the entire pan, otherwise blanks must be used to prevent the contents from floating around.   The lid is now attached and securely fastened, and by means of the crane the pan is swung in the metal.   It is allowed to float on the surface for about five minutes, or until thoroughly heated, when it is lowered slowly until completely submerged, and held there until the splashing and bubbling caused by the escaping steam ceases.   It is then gently raised to the surface and swung into the cooling box, the surface of which is covered with a thin layer of water. The metal will shrink as it cools, and the deficiency should be supplied with the ladle.   Cold metal will make defective casts. Cooling it too rapidly will cause cracks.   When cold, the pan is taken from the trough and laid on a strong bench or block. The iron clamp is loosened and the cover pried off with a cold-chisel.   The cast, which appears a solid lump of metal, is placed so that it lies in the same position as when in the pan, and the corners are struck with a heavy hammer until it separates in two parts, the molds and plate remaining attached to the metal. The plaster which adheres to the face of the cast may be removed by soaking in a trough of water. Casts are of an irregular thickness, and after being sawn to size are placed in an electrotypers' roughing machine and cut to the correct gauge. If all the operations have been carefully performed, the design will appear in low relief. Except where the lines are very close together, this will be insufficient for printing purposes. The large spaces must be removed in the routing machine, and the small ones carefully worked over with a graver. The block is then mounted on wood, when it is ready for use, but the metal being comparatively soft, it is always best to first make an electrotype.

INDEX.

www.ingramcontent.com/pod-product-compliance
Lightning Source LLC
Chambersburg PA
CBHW032008010726
47493CB00007B/2323